Roni paused, then flung her earrings, one after the other, as far as she could into the room. As a grand finale, she reached up and tore off her scarf, whirling it around her head. Zack played one more long, final drum roll, and as the cymbals clashed and the guitar went wild behind her, Roni flung the scarf out over the sea of people before her.

Suddenly Zack grabbed her, spinning her around the bandstand. "You're nuts, you know that?" Zack whispered in her ear, laughing.

"What did I tell you?" Roni said breathlessly as he set her down.

"I thought you were just trying to impress me."

Roni raised an eyebrow. "I did, didn't I?"

Zack shook his head at Roni in disbelief. "Are there any more like you at home?"

"There are none like me!" Roni exclaimed. "Anywhere." And from the looks on their faces, she knew Zack and his friends believed her.

Other books in the **ROOMMATES** series:

COMING SOON:

Roommates

EXTRA CREDIT
Alison Blair

BANTAM BOOKS
TORONTO · NEW YORK · LONDON · SYDNEY · AUCKLAND

EXTRA CREDIT

EXTRA CREDIT

A BANTAM BOOK   0 553 17574 2

First publication in Great Britain

PRINTING HISTORY
Bantam edition published 1988

Bantam Books are published by Transworld Publishers Ltd.,
61–63 Uxbridge Road, Ealing, London W5 5SA,
in Australia by Transworld Publishers (Australia) Pty. Ltd.,
15–23 Helles Avenue, Moorebank, NSW 2170, and in New
Zealand by Transworld Publishers (N.Z.) Ltd., Cnr. Moselle
and Waipareira Avenues, Henderson, Auckland.

Printed and bound in Great Britain by
Hazell Watson & Viney Limited
Member of BPCC plc
Aylesbury, Bucks, England

Chapter 1

"Vacation at last! I'm so excited I can't stand it." Roni Davies shielded her eyes from the Florida sun, which was already strong although it was only nine-thirty in the morning. She turned to her roommates in the backseat. "You know, you guys," Roni admitted, "I never thought we'd make it." She poked Stacy, who was driving, in the arm. "Don't miss our exit," she reminded her again.

Stacy grimaced as she maneuvered her silver-gray Mercedes into the passing lane.

"Stace, I just saw the sign for our exit," Roni said.

"I know. We have time." Stacy grinned patiently. "And I know you'll give me plenty of warning."

Roni leaned back. They'd been driving more than five hours. "Am I the only one who's excited?" She couldn't believe how calm Stacy was.

Sam piped up from the backseat. "Of course we're excited. You don't think we'll let you have all the fun, do you, Roni?"

"The truth?" Roni pushed her coppery-red hair away from her face and turned around. "I didn't think we'd make it here together. I thought Stacy would fly off to the Riviera or something, you'd spend the entire week on campus with Aaron, and Terry would be fixing up her new apartment. What a disaster! I could have ended up at home with my parents or something." She made a face. "Ugh! All that golf. Hanging out at the country club is their idea of a vacation."

Sam laughed. "Your parents can't be as bad as you make them out to be. Anyway, we all decided to follow your lead this time."

"My lead?" Roni looked mystified.

"Sure. Party all the time, fun in the sun—just your style, right?" Sam grinned devilishly.

Roni grinned back, then screamed, "Daytona Beach, next exit!" She whirled around in her seat. "Stacy, pull over or you'll miss it."

Roni reached for the steering wheel, but Stacy slapped at her hand. "Stop it. When I'm driving, I'll do the steering, okay? Just take it easy."

"But you missed the exit!"

"Have I made a mistake yet?" Coolly, Stacy accelerated and passed several cars. "There's another Daytona exit coming up."

In the backseat, Sam yawned and combed her fingers through her tousled, sun-bleached hair. "Take it easy, you two," she said good-naturedly. "I'll drive, if you want. It's my turn anyway."

"No way," Stacy said in her best, upper-class Boston accent. "I want to be at the wheel when we hit Daytona so I can make my grand entrance."

"Good. I'm too tired to see straight anyway." Sam yawned, glancing at their fourth roommate, Terry, who was sound asleep on the seat beside her.

"Terry's got the right idea. I wish I could nap like that."

"If you'd worked as hard as Terry did all semester, you'd be sleeping, too," Stacy said.

"All that work and now she's dropping out," Sam said, looking fondly at Terry. "It's kind of sad—our last trip together as roommates."

"And we're going to make every second count," Roni declared.

"Like starting off at the crack of dawn?" Stacy gave her a poisonous look. "Only farmers get up at four A.M."

"But we agreed," Roni protested. "Why waste a day traveling? This way, we won't miss a minute of sun."

"It sounded great until we actually had to do it," Stacy admitted, stifling a yawn. "Right now, I'd be glad to be back at school, sound asleep."

"You can sleep on the beach," Roni pointed out.

"I think I will." Stacy slowed down as she approached the exit ramp.

Roni felt a shiver of excitement run through her. Daytona Beach! No classes, no exams, no papers to write—nothing but fun and sun for a solid week. She could hardly wait. She wished Stacy would let her drive—not to steal away Stacy's "grand entrance," but just so she could feel in control of things, make everything happen even faster. She couldn't help saying, "Hurry, Stace."

Stacy winced at the nickname as she smoothly took a right turn onto a local street.

"Wait, you should have gone left!" Roni cried.

"Will you stop backseat driving?" Stacy warned, making another right turn.

"We should have gone left. I know it."

Sam peered out the window. "Hey, I think Roni's right. Don't our directions say left turns?"

"What's going on?" Terry suddenly piped up. "Where are we? I must have fallen asleep."

"Stacy's lost!" Roni cried. "Pull over, okay? I want to check the map." Roni got out their crumpled set of directions, scanning the paper hurriedly. "I know it said to turn left."

"I think Roni's right," Sam agreed. "The ocean's to the east of us, so we should turn left."

"I know what I'm doing," Stacy protested. "Trust me. I got us this far, didn't I?"

"Yeah, but I still say you should have turned left back there," Roni insisted. "We'll never get to the beach now."

"Cut it out, you guys." Terry clapped her hands over her ears.

"Then tell Roni to leave me alone and let me drive," Stacy snapped.

Suddenly everyone was arguing at once, and Roni felt like putting her hands over her ears, too. But then she saw something that changed her mind. "Look, you guys!" she yelled. "Look!"

Straight ahead was a strip of shimmering, turquoise-blue water. The ocean, at last!

"We're here! We're here!" Excitedly, Roni grabbed Stacy's arm and shook it hard.

"Fantastic!" Sam and Terry yelled at once.

Roni gazed around her in delight. "Just look at those palm trees, and that gorgeous blue water. It's even better than I thought it would be."

"Take it easy. It's not exactly the Riviera," Stacy drawled.

Roni laughed. "Maybe not, but how many of those exotic beaches are wall-to-wall college boys?" she asked, beaming. "Daytona Beach, here I come! Now who's complaining about getting up at four so we could spend the day on the beach?"

She tugged Stacy's arm. "Hey, stop! There's a parking space. Quick, grab it before someone else does."

Stacy slammed on the brakes and the car behind them stopped short, blasting its horn. Then it pulled around them.

Sam groaned loudly. "The excitement begins. Never a dull moment with Roni around."

Stacy craned her neck and looked down the street, then peered at Roni. "Why should I park here? I don't even see our motel."

"Who cares? We're practically *on* the beach, and I can't wait to start my tan. Who has the lotion, anyway?" Roni pulled up her skimpy crop top to reveal a skimpy green bikini top, which nearly glowed against her pale skin. "I didn't want to waste time changing," she explained.

"Sometimes, Veronica, you are too much," Stacy said, pulling the Mercedes back into traffic.

"What are you doing? That was a great parking space."

"Maybe, but I think I'll park at our motel."

"We can find it later," Roni insisted. "We're only going to sleep there, anyway." She gestured toward the crashing surf. "The ocean's only two feet away. We can't just leave it."

"It's not going anywhere," Stacy said.

Terry nodded in agreement. "We should buy some food and stuff. You know, I'm really glad we decided to get the room with the efficiency kitchen. This way, we won't have to spend all our money on restaurant meals."

Roni groaned. "Can't the food wait?"

"We have to check our room, too," Stacy pointed out. "You can't always trust these small-motel owners."

Sam added, "Yeah, and I need some things from the drugstore. But right after that," she said as Roni groaned again, "we'll definitely change into our suits and hit the beach."

"We'll be fast," Terry promised. "Ten minutes."

"Half an hour, tops," Sam said.

"Half an hour?" Roni felt like grumbling, but bit her tongue. Terry was not exactly the spontaneous type. She planned ahead for everything—which took away half the fun, as far as Roni was concerned.

An hour later, pushing a cart up and down the aisles of the Save-Mor Beach Mart, Roni was sorry she'd agreed to anything. She should have jumped out of the car and hit the beach alone. This was definitely not her idea of a good time.

She threw a pack of paper towels and two boxes of tissues into her cart, then turned the corner. In the next aisle, Terry and Sam stood elbow to elbow, examining a list of ingredients on a box of cereal.

"Nothing but sugar, preservatives, and chemicals!" Terry exclaimed. "No way." Yanking it out of Sam's hand, she put the box back on the shelf.

Roni reached up and tossed the box into her own cart. "Who cares!" she exclaimed, exasperated. "Forget about health food, okay? You can eat healthy cereal after vacation. Let's get out of here."

"This is taking longer than I thought," Sam said. "Maybe we should all buy food separately."

"It costs more that way," Terry reminded her.

Just then, Stacy hurried down the aisle, her hands full. "Look at these gorgeous steaks. We could have a fabulous cookout."

Roni gaped at her. "A cookout? We don't even have a barbecue grill."

"Sure we do. They have them on the beach. Besides," Stacy added slyly, "it's a perfect way to meet guys. We just say we need help getting the coals lit."

"I like the way you think," Roni replied, grabbing the steaks. Then, as she swung her cart in a wide arc, there was a crashing sound. "Oops, sorry." She had smashed right into a cart going the other way. "It was my fault."

"That's okay," said the girl pushing the other cart. She stared curiously at them all. "Excuse me, but . . . aren't you guys from Hawthorne College?"

Roni stared at the stranger, a delicate, fair-skinned girl with lovely blue eyes and long dark brown hair. "How did you know?"

"I go there, too." She turned to Sam. "You're Samantha Hill, aren't you? From my Shakespeare lecture."

Sam looked at the girl more closely. "Are you in that class?"

"Sure. Gosh, what a coincidence, seeing you here."

"You mean bumping into us," Roni corrected, joking.

"Yeah, I guess lots of Hawthorne kids come to Daytona for spring break," Sam said. "We all drove down this morning. Oh . . . uh . . . these are my roommates, Roni, Stacy, and Terry," she added, introducing them.

"I'm Maddie," the girl replied. "Madison, actually. Madison Lerner."

"Where are you staying?" Roni asked pleasantly.

"Oh . . . uh . . ." Maddie hesitated. "Just a little place up the beach."

"We're at the Surf Horizon," Roni told her, turning to leave. "Maybe we'll bump into you again."

"That'd be great," Maddie said eagerly. Then, as if to explain, she added, "I just transferred to Hawthorne, and I don't know very many people there yet."

"You should give Sam your phone number and make plans to get together," Roni suggested.

"Good idea," Sam agreed. She dug through her purse for a pencil and piece of paper.

Maddie hesitated. "Uh . . . why don't I call you instead? I . . . uh . . . never know when I'll be in my room. The Surf Horizon, right?"

"That's it," Sam told her.

"I've really got to go. Nice meeting you," Maddie told Roni, Terry, and Stacy before continuing down the aisle with her cart.

"That was strange," Sam murmured.

"Yeah, she seemed awfully anxious to make sure you didn't call her." Roni shook her head. "But she was really glad to see you. I don't get it."

"Who knows? Maybe she just needs a vacation."

Roni glanced at the jumble of packages in her cart and sighed. "I need a vacation, too, after all this shopping. Can't we just get this stuff for now and come back later for anything we missed?"

"Not a bad idea," Stacy agreed. "Let's hit the beach."

Terry hesitated. "Let's take a vote," she said. "All those in favor of getting all the important items on our list before we go to the beach, raise your hand."

Only Terry's hand went up. Roni, Stacy, and Sam glanced doubtfully at one another.

"I'd say you've been outvoted," Roni remarked with a giggle. "Sorry, Terry."

"Okay, I give up." Terry steered for the checkout counter. "But isn't it weird that the first person we meet in Daytona is from Hawthorne?"

"Yeah," Roni agreed. "Let's just hope the next person we meet is a guy—from anywhere."

Chapter 2

Roni rubbed suntan oil on her arms and shoulders and adjusted her sun visor. Beside her, Sam, Terry, and Stacy were sprawled on bright beach towels, checking the time every few minutes to make sure they wouldn't burn.

"This is the life," Stacy said as she rolled over to tan the sides of her legs. She accidentally kicked sand onto Roni's just-oiled legs.

"Look out!" Roni cried, and scraped sand off her skin. "Great. I've got sand all over me."

"Take it easy." Stacy was flipping through the pages of her favorite fashion magazine. "You've got to learn to relax."

"Relaxing is boring," Roni declared.

"Boring!" Terry opened her eyes and looked at her roommate in disbelief. "It's not boring, it's wonderful. Just smell that salt air."

"It's salty, all right," Roni admitted. "And the sun does feel great."

"Then stop complaining," Stacy told her. "Take a nap, read something—recharge your batteries."

Roni sat up. "But what if I fall asleep and miss the action?"

"What action?" Stacy scanned the beach. "Everyone's sunbathing. We'll find some action later, like around four."

"By then, I could have a pretty good base," Terry remarked, poking her thigh. A pale white dot appeared. "I'm already pink."

"If I have to lie here until then, I'll go stark, raving mad!" Roni exclaimed.

"If you need something to do, go find the nearest refreshment stand," Sam said lazily.

"Oooh. I'd kill for a cold drink," Stacy said. "The sodas we bought at the supermarket are still warm."

"Whoops! I forgot to get them out of the refrigerator section," Sam admitted.

Terry licked her lips. "I'd like a giant hot dog with all the trimmings."

"Me, too." Sam rolled her eyes. "And french fries. Or ice cream!"

"Okay! Okay!" Roni exclaimed. "I get the message. I volunteer for snack patrol. It'll be better than lying here. Terry, hand me my purse."

"Oh, no," Terry protested. "You and Stacy have treated all semester. This one's on me."

"No way. You're about to move into your own apartment. You'll need every penny," Roni said.

"But I'll also be working. Really, I can afford one treat."

"Well, okay." Roni grinned and took the crumpled bills from Terry as the other girls rolled over with contented sighs.

"Don't take too long," Stacy called, her voice muffled by her beach towel.

"I'll hurry. What else is there to do?"

The sand was hot under Roni's feet as she walked up the beach. She almost turned back for her rubber thongs, but the refreshment stand couldn't be very far away. And anyway, the beach was so beautiful and colorful that she soon forgot her burning feet. Hundreds of brightly clad bodies were stretched out on towels on the clean, white sand, and radios were playing everywhere. Palm trees lined the narrow strip of beach, looking dramatic against the deep blue sky. It was gorgeous, all right, but the hundreds of cute guys scattered over the beach were even better scenery. Some boys who looked as if they were still in high school stared at her, but Roni gave them the cold shoulder. She was hardly interested in robbing the cradle. There were also a few groups of older men there—guys in their late twenties or even thirties. They were acting half their ages—something Roni absolutely detested. Who needed some old guy who couldn't keep up with you?

All she wanted was a little attention from someone who was cute and her age.

And her bright green bikini was attracting plenty of attention, she noticed with satisfaction. It was the latest style—very skimpy and definitely sexy.

Roni tugged at her bright yellow visor and smoothed back her hair, which she had braided over one shoulder for the occasion. The combination of her auburn braid and her sensational bikini made up for her completely pale skin. And even that wouldn't be a problem much longer. The sun was so hot, she'd be tan in no time.

Roni smiled with satisfaction as an incredibly hunky guy stood up and stretched right in front of her, flexing his impressive muscles. It was quite a show, and obviously for her benefit. Grateful for her dark sunglasses, she gave him a quick once-over. A tiny bikini bathing suit showed off every gleaming inch of his perfectly tanned skin. This guy believed in perfection. Even his hair was perfect. *Definitely uses mousse*, Roni thought regretfully.

This guy had his look down, all right—proving he was just the type to spend more time thinking about himself than about her. She threw him a tiny grin but turned away, making her way past some other blankets. Luckily, Mr. Perfect wasn't the only guy who was looking her way. A guy in an Ohio State T-shirt offered her a soda as she passed, and two Ivy League types were battling each other to get to her first. Roni didn't bother stopping to talk to anyone, though. After all, with this many guys around and nothing but free time, she could take her pick.

But first, the refreshment stand. "Finally!" she exclaimed, spotting it across the street. It seemed as if she'd been walking for blocks. Just as she stepped off the curb, a carload of guys in a red convertible spotted her. Wolf whistles filled the air. The convertible swerved to follow Roni as she crossed to the opposite sidewalk. Another few inches and the car would have been up on the sidewalk.

"What are you trying to do?" she yelled, barely holding back a burst of giggles. This was the kind of action she'd hoped to find. Who cared about sun-bathing, anyway?

"Since when is driving allowed on the side-walks?" a girl with a headful of bleached-blonde hair asked, staring at Roni.

"Since that girl started walking on them," her friend quipped.

Roni got in line behind two girls and tried to ignore them, but the blonde continued to stare at her.

"You must be wearing a magnet or something," she said.

"Yeah, the wrong kind of magnet," Roni quipped. "They were cute, but definitely not my style."

"Oh? What *is* your style?" the girl asked.

Roni put on a thick Southern accent, saying, "Why, I was raised to think a gentlemen should respect a lady." She dropped the pose. "I know better now."

They both laughed. "You sound like a genuine Southern belle," the blonde commented. "Where are you from?"

"Georgia. And proud of it. I go to Hawthorne College. It's a really small school right outside Atlanta."

"Never heard of it." Rudely, the girl turned away. "Can you imagine going to school somewhere as awful as Atlanta?" Roni heard her say to her friend. "I'll bet only geeks go there."

"Hey, Hawthorne is a *great* school!" Roni ex-claimed. "Just because you've never heard of it . . ."

The girls ignored her. Steaming, Roni took a deep breath, about to give them a real piece of her mind.

But just then, someone tapped her on the shoulder.

"Did you say you go to Hawthorne?"

Roni whirled around. A dark-haired girl with wild curls stood beside her.

"And what if I do?" Roni snapped.

The dark-haired girl eyed her curiously. "Nothing. You just don't look like the Hawthorne type."

"Oh! Yeah, I guess I know what you mean," Roni said. "There are so many prim and proper little ladies there—too many. I'm not one of them," Roni assured her.

"Good. I'm sick to death of wholesome, rah-rah types. That's why I came down here—to get away from them."

"Me, too," Roni said.

The girl squinted and smiled at her. "I'm Lisa Evans," she said. "And this is my friend, Mary Lou Franklin. We're juniors at Hawthorne."

Roni's mouth dropped open. "Hi, I'm Roni Davies," she answered, "and I don't believe you go to my school!"

The boy at the window took Roni's order, and she had to concentrate to remember everything. Meanwhile, Lisa, who had gotten half her order, waited beside her. She stuck a straw in a soda and took a long sip.

"Who are you here with, anyway? I'm with a bunch of other Hawthorne juniors."

"Juniors, huh?" Roni hadn't met many Hawthorne upperclassmen—they didn't seem to notice freshmen. She frowned, not wanting to give herself away. "Oh, just some friends."

Lisa frowned. "I thought I knew everybody. I

wonder why I haven't seen you on campus. I'd definitely notice you."

"Oh, well, I haven't been around much. I . . . uh . . . just transferred." She probably should have admitted the truth, but she knew Lisa's type. As soon as she found out Roni was a freshman, she'd have no time left to talk. But if Roni played it right, Lisa might be very helpful. She'd probably been to Daytona before, which meant she knew where to find the real action.

"Gee, that's a fantastic suit," Roni told Lisa.

Lisa's suit was one-piece, hot pink and blazing yellow. It swept up over one shoulder, and had an uneven triangle cutout on the stomach and another low in the back. It wasn't really *flattering*, Roni thought, but very attention-getting. Definitely attention-getting.

Lisa glanced at Roni's outfit and then down at her own. "I thought I'd really stand out in this," she confided, "but now I'm sorry I ever got it."

"How come? It's great-looking," Roni said sincerely.

"Yeah, but you see, I brought this really killer sundress with me. It's blue and white and cut real low in the back. I didn't realize, though—if I get a tan, I'll have a giant triangle right in the middle of my back. And I'm definitely getting a tan."

Roni frowned. "Oh, that is a problem," she admitted. "Hey, I know—I've got two extra suits with me. In fact, one is a dynamite red bikini that would look fabulous with your dark hair. I'll bet we're the same size, too. You could borrow it."

"You don't even know me."

Roni shrugged. "We're classmates, aren't we?"

Lisa frowned. "Okay, but I don't want to wear anything boring and ordinary," she warned.

"This suit is hardly ordinary," she said, annoyed. Lisa sure wasn't much on gratitude. "And nothing I own is boring."

Lisa's dark eyes narrowed. "I believe you. You're definitely not like everyone else."

"Lis—here's the rest of our order." Mary Lou handed a tray of drinks and snacks to Lisa. "We'd better hurry. The guys were dying of thirst."

Impatiently, Lisa picked up a tray. There was still one more on the counter. "We'll never be able to carry all this." She looked at Roni hopefully. "Hey, how about helping out?"

Roni's order was packed into a single paper bag. She could easily carry it and still manage a tray. "Sure, I'll help. Where's your blanket?"

Lisa grinned. "It's not exactly a blanket," she said mysteriously.

Curious, Roni followed her down the narrow beach. They were heading in the opposite direction from her roommates.

"Not too much farther," Lisa called.

"Lis," Mary Lou whispered a little too loudly, "are you inviting her along?"

Lisa grinned at Roni, then looked at Mary Lou. "Why not? I think Roni seems like fun."

Roni couldn't help feeling pleased, even though they were girls. If she didn't start meeting some guys pretty soon, this vacation would be a total bust.

"There's our stuff," Lisa said, pointing across the beach.

"Wow! Some blanket!" Roni stopped in surprise. Lisa's friends had strung up a huge canvas tarp between two tall poles, making a kind of tent. On one side was a giant square of shade, and there was a bright area of sunlit sand on the other. At least a dozen people were lounging on towels around a giant picnic cooler.

"Help has arrived," Lisa called gaily, lifting her tray in the air.

A good-looking guy with longish brown hair ran up to her. "What took you so long?"

"This is Ray," Lisa proudly told Roni. "He's gorgeous, but he's also mine. Just telling you to avoid complications."

"Or competition," Mary Lou cracked. Lisa bumped her playfully with the tray.

Ray nodded toward Roni. "Who's the mystery girl?"

Lisa shrugged coyly. "We don't really know," she teased. "It's a mystery, and you'll have to solve it yourself."

"Well, then, let's get our expert puzzle man over here. Hey, Zack," Ray said, kicking up sand next to a stocky boy who was dozing nearby. "Wake up."

"Watch it!" Zack brushed sand off his face. Then he spied Roni and sat up. Smiling in appreciation, he asked, "Who's this?"

"Ah, it's a mystery," Lisa told him. "You have to find out for yourself."

Roni was looking at Zack. She couldn't believe she'd never noticed him around school. She would have remembered that dusty-brown hair and those clear gray eyes. What a hunk!

"A mystery, huh?" Zack nodded thoughtfully. "Let me hear you talk," he demanded.

Roni did her best imitation of a Boston accent. "What should I say?"

"Aha! A northeastern girl, right?"

"He's right," Lisa gasped, winking at Roni.

Zack looked surprised. "I am?"

"That's amazing," Roni said, gazing into Zack's eyes. "Guess some more."

"You go to school in New England."

Was she crazy, or did he look disappointed?

Lisa started to say something, but Roni quickly cut her off. "I go to Hawthorne," she blurted out, dropping the phony accent.

Zack grinned. "That's good news."

"But she's not your typical Hawthorne girl," Lisa told him. "If she was, I wouldn't have picked her out of the crowd."

"Is that what happened?"

"You got it," Roni said. "We met at the refreshment stand."

"You have good taste in women," Zack told Lisa as his eyes met Roni's. She felt herself blush. "She's not ordinary at all."

"That's what my daddy always told me," Roni said playfully. "He's a senator."

"Your father's a senator?" Lisa looked impressed.

"Uh, yes, he is," Roni said modestly. "I hate it when people make a fuss over it, though." She was thinking of Stacy's Beacon Hill pedigree, and wondering how she would have let Zack know she was a senator's daughter.

Zack's eyebrows rose in surprise. "I would never have guessed that."

Roni lifted her head haughtily, imitating Stacy's most aristocratic pose. "I won't hold that against you," she quipped.

Zack smiled, making Roni's heart beat faster. "You mean you'll still talk to a commoner like me."

"You're hardly a commoner," Lisa reminded him. "His father's no senator, but he's pretty well off."

"Oh? Maybe we should get to know each other." Roni eyed him flirtatiously. "If I'd known you then, I'd have invited you to my debutante party." That part wasn't even a lie—she was presented at a debutante ball. Only it was in Atlanta, not Boston.

"At least she's not after your money, Cooper," Ray broke in, looking at Zack.

"Zack Cooper. That's a great name," Roni told him.

"I bet yours is great, too."

"Roni, short for Veronica."

"No fair!" Lisa exclaimed. "He's supposed to guess!"

Roni giggled. "You can't guess someone's name!" she cried.

"Why not? Hey, let's try to guess one another's middle names." Lisa sat down and the others sat with her in a circle. As they played, Roni stole quick glances at Zack. He had a fabulous body and a terrific profile.

She liked Lisa and her friends a lot—especially Zack. Roni knew she would have a great time with them. They weren't boring; anyone could see that.

"I'm still starved," Ray announced suddenly. "Isn't there any more food?"

"Food!" Roni exclaimed. "I forgot all about the stuff I bought for my roommates."

"It's been awhile," Lisa remarked.

"Yeah, they probably got something else to eat by now." Roni hesitated, then grabbed the bag and handed it to Ray, who took it greedily.

"Oh, well," she said lightly. "I hope that's enough for you."

"It'll do for now," he said, "but what about dinner?"

Mary Lou nodded in agreement. "Yeah, what's going on tonight?"

Lisa shrugged. "I don't know. I'm fresh out of ideas." She turned suddenly to Roni. "Do you know of anything fun we could do tonight?"

"Me?" Roni glanced at Zack, then grinned at Lisa in delight. "I always know what to do."

Chapter 3

Roni heard shrieks of pain as she turned her key in the motel room door.

"Stop, you're killing me!" Terry cried as Roni entered the room.

"What's going on? Terry, what happened to you?"

Terry looked up from the couch, where she was lying with her face on a towel as Sam swabbed her back and shoulders.

"What's that?" Roni asked, coming closer. "It smells awful."

"Vinegar," Sam said. "Terry was out in the sun a little too long. This will keep it from blistering."

"How long did you guys stay out there?" Roni asked, staring at the blazing sunburn on Terry's back and legs.

Stacy gave Roni a funny look. "You'd know if you hadn't gone off somewhere. What happened to you, anyway?"

"Oh, I met these great people," Roni began. "And you'll never believe it—they're from Hawthorne! There's this girl Lisa and her boyfriend, Ray, and a really cute guy named Zack Cooper. And Mary Lou, and Evelyn. . . . I forget the other kids' names. They're all juniors and seniors."

"That's great, but we thought you were coming back. I mean, you just took Terry's money and disappeared," Stacy said.

"I'm really sorry," Roni said. She dug through the shelf under the wooden divider that served as their kitchenette and came up with bag of cookies. "I got involved and just forgot."

Terry turned over, wincing as her shoulder brushed the rough upholstery of the couch. "That's okay. I've had enough sun for one day, anyway."

"This room is no great prize," Stacy commented. "I've stayed in some places with better pets' quarters."

Roni glanced around. The walls were covered in false-pine paneling instead of the cheery white stucco she'd expected to find at a Florida resort. Scuffed linoleum covered the floors, the furniture was on its last legs, and the prints on the walls were cheap and ugly.

"It's not that bad," Terry said, trying to sound positive.

"Oh, no? It isn't even half as nice as our suite at school."

Terry frowned. "Maybe. But it was the best we could afford as a group."

"I know," Stacy said quickly. "I didn't mean to complain, really. I guess I'm just annoyed because . . ." She flushed and didn't say anything more.

"Because of me," Roni finished for her.

"Well, yes. If you were having such a great time, you could have come and gotten us," Stacy said.

"Actually, I wasn't anywhere near you." Roni gestured helplessly. "I'm sorry, guys. Come on, we came here to have fun, and I was just having fun."

"It's no big deal," Sam said peaceably. "We'll all probably meet people."

"That reminds me," Roni remarked, perching on the edge of the sofa. "I saw your friend Maddie on my way back here." She paused dramatically. "And she wasn't alone."

"Who was she with?" Sam asked. "Hawthorne students?"

"Not even close." Roni grinned devilishly. "Something tells me I underestimated that girl."

"What do you mean?"

"She seemed like the shy, quiet type, right?"

"She is, pretty much," Sam agreed. "But she seems really nice in class."

"Well, she's not so shy after all." Roni's eyes danced wickedly. "Madison Lerner . . . is dating an older man."

"What? What are you saying?" Sam and Stacy crowded onto the couch next to Roni.

"I was just leaving the beach with Lisa and her friends, and I noticed this couple. We all noticed"— she gave a short laugh—"because they had this horrendous fight. They were yelling about something. Then the woman stomped off and the man yelled after her, 'Oh, really?' Then, a few minutes later, who comes strolling down the beach but your friend Maddie!"

"She's not exactly my friend," Sam corrected.

"Anyway, this guy starts talking to Maddie, and before you know it, he's rolled up his blanket and the two of them walked off together—arm in arm!"

"I don't believe it," Sam said.

Stacy shrugged. "That could mean anything."

"Give me a break," Roni insisted. "I know what I saw. They were *very* friendly."

"What did the guy look like?" Sam asked, frowning. "I mean, what if she's in some kind of trouble? Maybe we should check and see if she's okay."

"We can't," Roni answered. "She wouldn't tell us her motel, remember? Now we know why—she's fooling around with a married man and doesn't want anyone to know."

Sam looked stunned. "That would explain why she acted so funny," she said. "It could be true, I suppose."

"Believe it," Roni told her. "The guy has some nerve, too, picking a fight with his wife to get rid of her."

Sam shook her head sadly. "Poor Maddie, if she's mixed up in something like that." She sighed. "Oh, well, I guess we won't be hearing from her again."

"You never know," Stacy said wisely. "She might have a lot of time on her hands, waiting for him to have another fight with his wife."

Sam shook her head. "I hate the whole thing," she said. "Let's talk about something else."

"How about dinner?" Terry suggested. "Let's all do something special—you know, to mark our first night here."

"I read about a great place in that brochure we got," Stacy said enthusiastically. "It's a comedy club—five-dollar cover, no minimum, and they don't check ID's."

"Perfect!" Terry cried. "Let's go there. I might never have a chance like this again."

"Come on, you'll have weekends off on your new job, won't you?" Sam asked. "And what about vacations? Everyone gets vacations eventually."

"I might not. I'll just have to play it by ear."

Sam let out a whoop. "You're the last person on the face of the earth to play things by ear, and you know it. Didn't you even ask about vacations?"

"No," Terry admitted, embarrassed. "I was so happy to get a job at a TV station, I would have paid them." Everyone laughed, including Terry. "I still get nervous when I think about it—leaving school and all. I know I'll miss my classes, and you guys, of course."

"The way I miss Aaron," added Sam wistfully. "I can't believe he had to stay at school and work."

Roni rolled her eyes. "This is getting depressing. Come on, you guys, we're on vacation!"

"Roni's right," Sam said, smiling. "Let's get this party in gear."

"Oh," Roni said. "Uh . . . I sort of made plans to eat with Lisa's friends tonight."

"You didn't!" Terry cried in disappointment.

"Well . . . uh . . . maybe you guys could come along," Roni suggested. "That'd be nice."

Terry looked doubtful. "Wouldn't they mind?"

Stacy held up a hand. "No way. I don't want to crash somebody else's party. But you go ahead. Really. We can always meet your friends tomorrow."

"Sure," Roni agreed quickly. "There's always tomorrow. No matter what, let's spend the whole day together, okay?"

Terry brightened. "And let's take a really long walk down the beach—for miles. I want to see every inch of Daytona."

"I'll go along with that." Sam nodded.

"It's a date." Roni beamed.

Stacy insisted that Terry and Sam dress up for their first evening out. The vinegar had helped Terry's sunburn, and she looked smashing in a light cotton sweater and tan pants. Roni spent a few frantic minutes advising everyone on finishing touches—earrings, belts, makeup. They all looked terrific, tan, and very summery. But by the time Roni saw them out, she barely had time to get dressed herself.

Lisa and her friends were either going to hit some disco, or maybe just party on the beach— they really weren't sure. Roni decided to play it safe, pulling on a red tank suit and placing a pair of yellow cotton pants over it. She'd take the pants off if they went near the water, or she'd just keep the pants on and roll them up. She slipped on a matching yellow shirt, letting the red tank show at the neck. If they did go dancing, she could just pull off the shirt and still look great. And no one would ever guess it was a bathing suit—if that even mattered down here. From the stories she'd heard, she wouldn't have been surprised if people went dancing barefoot and in bikinis.

Shaking out her braid, Roni let her hair ripple naturally around her shoulders. She used less

makeup than usual, so that if they did go swimming, her mascara and eye shadow wouldn't get all
smudged under her eyes. She decided to leave it
simple, but at the last minute she couldn't resist
tying a sparkly fringed red scarf around her head,
making a floppy bow over one ear. Finally, she was
ready to go, and headed downstairs to wait.

"Roni—over here!"

As soon as she stepped out the front door, Roni
saw Lisa waving wildly from a dark green Jeep
parked at the curb. Roni hurried over, grinning
broadly. "Great car! Whose is it?"

"Zack's," Lisa said grandly. "Of course, this is just
his play car. He has another one at home for formal
occasions."

Roni rolled her eyes. Besides Lisa, Zack, and Ray,
Roni recognized Mary Lou and Evelyn, a tall
blonde, from the beach that day. The guys all
seemed to be wearing shorts and cotton shirts. Lisa
had on a form-fitting, cotton-knit dress—a black
outfit that set off her dramatic coloring. Mary Lou
and Evelyn were both wearing cotton pants. Roni
fit in, but she wished she'd been more daring—
worn her own short romper, the bright turquoise
one with big bows at the shoulders.

Roni counted four guys and, including herself,
four girls—just right to split up into couples. Lisa
was with Ray, but she couldn't figure out the other
twosomes. As Roni was checking it out, Mary Lou
pushed over in the backseat.

"You have to sit on someone's lap," Mary Lou told
her. "Zack's rule—he can't stand driving with
someone crowding his shifting arm."

"He's right," Ray said. "Zack's a serious driver. No more than three up front, ever."

"Well, excuse me," Roni said flippantly to cover her hurt feelings. So much for hitting it off with Zack. Dutifully, she climbed in the back between Mary Lou and Steve. Sitting on the edge of the seat and resting her arms on the front seat, she said, "I'll fit in fine here."

"Great." Zack turned around, giving her an extra-wide smile. "So, where are we going?"

"I thought you knew," Lisa said. "You're driving."

"Oh, no. I'm not making the decisions for this crew." Zack put his hands up in front of himself.

"I heard about this great comedy club," Roni offered.

"Sounds fun, but I don't really want to sit around listening," Zack told her. "I need some action."

"Carbonella's!" someone exclaimed. "It's the hottest dance club in Daytona."

"All right!" Zack put the Jeep in gear and pulled away from the curb, tires screeching.

"Where is this place?" Roni yelled above the noise of the engine.

"Not far," Zack yelled back.

"Not the way you drive," Lisa joked, pushing her hair out of her face.

"What?" Roni leaned over to hear.

"She thinks I'm a wild driver!" Zack screamed.

"I can't hear you!"

"Come up front if you want to hear," Zack told her.

Roni grinned. "Okay." Throwing one leg over the front seat, she started to climb over just as Zack swerved around to pass another car. Roni grabbed his shoulder to steady herself, but just then Zack reached up and tugged her shoulder. Roni spilled crazily onto Lisa's lap.

"You are a wild one!" Zack yelled, laughing.

"Hey, you told me to do it," Roni said as she squeezed in next to Lisa.

"Do you do everything people tell you to do?"

"Sure, if it's fun."

Lisa leaned over Roni and poked Zack in the arm. "Hey, what about your rule against four in front?"

"Roni just broke it," Zack said with a shrug.

Roni braced one arm against the dashboard as Zack yelled, "Hold on, everybody!" The Jeep tore down the wide street, and Roni threw her head back, letting the wind whip through her hair, the red scarf flapping crazily against her face.

"Want any?" Ray nudged her, and Roni noticed he was holding a bottle hidden in a paper bag.

"What's that?"

"Beer. Keep it out of sight," Zack warned. "If the cops see us driving with that, our party days are over."

"Then I'd better get rid of the evidence," Ray said, tipping the bottle to his mouth. He drank and passed the bottle to Lisa, who took a sip and passed it on to Roni.

"Ugh, it's warm." Roni wiped her mouth and passed the bottle back to Lisa.

Over the noise of the Jeep, Zack said, "I bet you're not like this back at school. You're probably Miss Prim and Proper."

"Not me," she assured him. "But at school, it

doesn't take much to be daring." She elbowed him teasingly, tossing her hair. "I always say, do whatever you want. Who cares what people think?"

"Do you really believe that?"

Roni tossed her head defiantly. "Of course."

Zack glanced at her as if he didn't quite believe her. Then he gunned the engine and pulled ahead suddenly, throwing everyone back against their seats.

The sky wasn't quite dark, but in front of Carbonella's, bright pink, blue, and amber spotlights played against the stucco building, highlighting the name of the club. Four pairs of palm trees on the sidewalk in front of the club were also illuminated with spotlights. Roni had never seen such an exciting-looking place. Everything about the night felt special—the summery air, the clear cloudless sky. Or maybe it was just the relaxed, warm feeling left over from a day in the sun.

Everyone piled out of the Jeep. Evelyn put her arms through Mark's as Zack took both Mary Lou and Lisa by the hand, pulling them through the door with him. Roni stared at them for a second, then grabbed Ray and Steve, linking arms with one boy on each side of her. She wished Zack would look back and see she had two escorts also.

They stopped at the door, where a rough-looking guy collected five dollars each from them and stamped their hands with ink that glowed under the bright lights. Up ahead, Roni could see a medium-sized room that was already packed with kids. A small, raised stage stood at the far end of the place, with CARBONELLA'S spelled out in splashy, pulsing neon over it.

Roni swept grandly down the three shallow steps, tossing adoring looks first at Ray, then at Steve. She let out an exaggerated laugh as they sat down at two small tables, which Zack had pushed together. "Great place," she commented.

Zack didn't seem to have noticed her grand entrance. Without even looking at her, he ordered drinks all around. Before their drinks arrived, he got up and pulled first Lisa, and then Mary Lou, up to dance with him. Roni noticed with disappointment that he didn't sit down until the break—and he didn't pay any attention to her. She was pretty busy herself, though, asking Mark and Steve as well as a few other boys to dance. She only stopped when Lisa waved at her from the table.

"Try one of these," Lisa said as Roni sat down beside her. She pushed over a frothy, exotic-looking drink. Roni took a long sip.

"Not bad," she said. "You can hardly tell there's any liquor in it."

"That way you can drink more," Lisa answered, grinning.

Zack came back to the table just then. "Wow, I'm pooped. Great band, huh?"

"Yeah, terrific," Roni agreed in a cool tone. "Between Ray, Mark, and Steve, I haven't had a chance to sit down."

"I saw you," Zack said, "dancing with anyone you could find."

"Why not? The music's great." Roni frowned. She really wanted to dance with Zack, but how could she get him to ask her? The waiter came by, and she ordered a drink like Lisa's.

"I was in a club like this once in the south of France," she said, recalling a story Stacy had told her about a fabulous disco on the Riviera.

"With the senator?" Lisa looked interested.

"He loves to take fancy vacations," Roni told her. "Always the best places, no expense spared. First class all the way."

"Must be nice." Lisa sighed.

"Sometimes," Roni agreed with a shrug. "You get tired of fancy things after a while, though. All the expensive gifts in the world can't make you happy."

"They don't hurt," Lisa countered dryly.

"I mean it," Roni said quietly. "After a while, you get used to the luxuries." She frowned, thinking of her own privileged childhood. Somehow, even with all her toys and clothes, she'd always wanted something more. She just didn't know what it was.

Lisa teased Roni. "You're only saying that so we won't be jealous."

"I don't think so." Zack rose to her defense. "Roni has a . . . a sensitive streak," he said finally.

Surprised, Roni lowered her eyes. She didn't really want things to get so heavy. But Zack reached over, gently touching the back of her hand.

Roni couldn't tear her eyes away from his. So Zack liked the sensitive type. She felt like an actress in a tragic play and heard the words tumbling from her mouth before she could think. "I didn't think it showed," she whispered. "It's . . . it's just my father. . . ." She hesitated, then went on. "He doesn't *mean* to drink so much, but ... well, he can't help himself sometimes."

"Poor kid," Zack muttered.

"That's why I said money can't buy happiness. I should know." Her drink came and she sipped it eagerly, glad to take a break from her storytelling.

Zack lifted his own glass. "Shouldn't you take it easy? I mean, with your father and all ... Aren't you worried?"

Roni peered into her glass as if she were peering into her painful past. "Sometimes I drink to ... uh ... to forget."

Lisa chortled. "Forget what? That weird guy you danced with last?"

A haunted, dreamy expression came to Roni's face. She actually felt a dull, aching loss, and she let herself look deep into Zack's eyes with a challenging yet tragic glance. "I wish it was that." She sighed. "Never mind, it's not a happy story."

Zack looked concerned. "Look, if something is really troubling you ..."

"I'm used to feeling this way," Roni told them. She noticed Zack was watching her intently. "It's been"—her voice broke—"almost three years now." She could feel everyone at the table watching her. It was so easy to get their attention this way—easy, and fun.

Zack moved closer, blocking out the others. "Three years? Since what?"

Roni closed her eyes, looking as if she were unable to face a very painful memory. "The accident," she barely whispered. "My brother was the oldest."

Zack stared.

Roni kept her eyes down. By now she almost believed it. The accident that had killed Terry's older brother seemed to have happened to her brother, a brother she didn't even have in real life. When she didn't answer right away, Zack took her hand and stroked it, gently squeezing her fingers.

"I'm sorry," he said in a soft voice.

She said quietly, "In a strange way, it's made me . . . more demanding. I mean, I don't settle for doing anything halfway now. Because you never know. Just live for today," she added seriously. "That's what you've got to do."

"I understand. The memories must still be painful."

"Don't get me wrong, I have standards—high ones."

"Meaning what?" Zack prompted.

Roni was talking about herself now, not borrowing facts from Terry's life, or Stacy's. "Meaning I never take less than exactly what I want."

They sat there silently for a while before Zack said, "Tell me what you're thinking."

She arched an eyebrow comically. "I'm thinking of all the ways my parents tried to get me to behave."

"Did any of them work?"

"None," she said. Roni lifted her eyes to meet Zack's. As they examined each other's faces, she felt suddenly shaken. Everything was closing in on her. She leaped up.

"This silence is deafening!" she exclaimed. "Where's the band?"

"You want music?" Without warning, Zack jumped to his feet and bounded onto the stage. Before Roni knew what was happening, he sat down at the drums and started a long drum roll.

"Let's party!" he shouted.

"What *is* he doing?" Ray asked, laughing.

Lisa began to clap. "Come on, Zack, show them you really know how to play."

To Roni's amazement, Zack started tapping out a long, complicated drum riff. Almost instantly, the lead guitarist appeared at his side, looking angry. Zack merely saluted and kept right on playing. Finally, the guitarist picked up his guitar and began to play along, improvising.

Roni's mouth dropped open. "He's really good," she blurted out. "I don't believe it."

"Incredible, but true," Lisa agreed, looking amazed.

Zack and the guitarist were really into it. Soon the other musicians came back onstage and they all began to play, taking their cues from one another. After a while, the music turned more suggestive and the crowd loved it. At their table, a wide smile spread across Ray's face.

"That's perfect music for a striptease," he said.

"Then do one," Lisa dared him. "I certainly won't."

"They'd throw me out," he answered. He gazed at Roni. "Hey, society girl—what would your father the senator think if his daughter did a striptease down in Florida? Come on, I dare you."

"Leave her alone, Ray," Mary Lou said.

Roni smiled crookedly. "You don't think I have the nerve?"

"Not in a million years," Ray said, shaking his head.

"Oh, yeah? Just watch me." In a flash, Roni scrambled onto the stage, grabbing the microphone. "Hello, Daytona Beach," she called.

In front of her, she could see Lisa's shocked face. Everyone at her table was staring in surprise.

"Go for it, Roni!" Ray yelled.

Behind her, Zack was drumming his heart out.

Light-headed and feeling reckless, Roni started dancing as she'd never danced before. She could feel the excitement in the room as she whirled around the stage, hypnotized by the driving rhythm of the music.

"Take it off!" Ray yelled. The others quickly joined in, laughing and cheering.

Roni unbuttoned the top few buttons of her yellow shirt, flashing her red bathing suit underneath. The crowd screamed with laughter. Egged on, Roni undid the rest of the buttons and flung the shirt open. She pulled it loose and whirled it over her head. The band was going crazy. Finally, Roni let the shirt go, and it sailed over everyone's heads, spinning into the crowd.

Lisa caught the shirt and waved it triumphantly over her head. By now, everyone was cheering wildly. People were screaming and shouting. Some of the guys, especially the ones who'd had a lot to drink, were begging Roni to take it all off. But most of the crowd was howling with laughter, and everyone was clapping wildly.

Behind her, Zack shook his head in disbelief. Roni threw him a daring look. Really into it now, she swung her hips and danced with abandon across the stage. She lifted a leg and kicked her foot, sending her shoe flying into the crowd. Someone caught it and held it up like a prize. Her other shoe went after it.

Roni paused, then flung her earrings, one after the other, as far as she could into the room. As a grand finale, she reached up and tore off her scarf, whirling it around her head. Zack played one more long, final drum roll, and as the cymbals clashed and the guitar went wild behind her, Roni flung the scarf out over the sea of people before her.

Suddenly Zack grabbed her, spinning her around the bandstand. The place went wild.

"You're nuts, you know that?" Zack whispered in her ear, laughing.

"What did I tell you?" Roni said breathlessly as he set her down.

"I thought you were just trying to impress me."

Roni raised an eyebrow. "I did, didn't I?"

Zack nodded and hoisted her in his arms, carrying her back to their table, where he set her back on her chair. He turned to Lisa. "Where did you find this girl?"

"No place special," Lisa said.

Zack shook his head at Roni in disbelief. "Are there any more like you at home?"

"There are none like me!" Roni exclaimed. "Anywhere." And from the looks on their faces, she knew Zack and his friends believed her.

Chapter 4

Roni's head was splitting as she forced herself to wake up. Turning on her side, she saw the twin bed across the room was empty. She couldn't believe it—Terry even got up early on vacation! Probably out jogging or something. Roni groaned just thinking about it. She pressed her hands against her temples to stop the throbbing. What she needed was a good, strong cup of coffee—maybe even a *pot* of coffee!

Sunlight streamed through the flimsy curtains in the living room. Squinting, Roni closed them. She got some water and started the coffee, then dropped onto the couch. Idly, she picked up the box of chocolates someone had left on the coffee table and popped one into her mouth. It was fabulous.

Surprised, she focused her eyes on the box. *Chocolatier de Paris*, it read. *Miami Beach, Fort Lauderdale, Daytona*. Taking another piece, she noticed two huge floor cushions propped against the sofa. She sank onto one of them. Perfect— cushy and cozy, just right for curling into for a lazy morning. Next to her, a giant bamboo fan leaned against the end table. Absently, she began to fan herself. It was already hot enough for air conditioning.

Funny, she hadn't seen those cushions and fan before. She yawned luxuriously and suddenly her eyes popped open. Wait a minute! This wasn't her room! She scrambled to her feet, a queasy feeling in the pit of her stomach. Where was she? All these motel rooms looked exactly alike—how could she tell if she was in the right one? She'd had so much to drink the night before. Had some guy taken her to his motel and now she didn't even remember it?

She felt sick to her stomach. But who? Zack! A smile formed on her lips and she felt a flutter of excitement. Had Zack actually taken her home with him? Did he like her? Damn! She ought to remember something that important! If only she didn't have this stupid hangover she could think straight. What had Zack said to her last night? She couldn't have forgotten, could she?

But what if . . . she didn't want to think about it? But what if it wasn't Zack at all? What if she'd gone home with someone else, a stranger, someone she wouldn't even remember if she saw him again? Her heart began to beat faster and she felt all sweaty. How drunk had she gotten last night, anyway? There was a sudden noise at the front door and Roni stiffened. Idiotically, she lifted the bamboo fan overhead, as if she could defend herself with it.

When she heard the voices on the other side of the door, she was so relieved that she had an attack of the giggles. What an imagination!

"Don't tell me you're just getting up!" Terry

dropped a carton of groceries on the coffee table.

"Ouch! Quietly," Roni said, pointing to her head. "Hangover."

"It's past eleven," Sam whispered. "We've been up for hours."

"Obviously. The question is: Why?" Roni wanted to know.

"Habit, I guess. We finished up the shopping from yesterday," Sam said as Terry brought in two more full bags from outside. "Stacy already hit the beach. She said she'd leave you a note so you wouldn't freak."

"I did freak," Roni admitted. "For a minute I wasn't even sure this was the right motel room. They all look alike, you know."

"Yeah, crummy," Sam said with a laugh.

"I didn't think to look for a note." Roni pulled a box of doughnuts from one of the paper bags.

"Hey, those are for lunch."

"I'll eat anything."

Terry lifted the box of candies and peeked inside. "I'll say. Pretty rich breakfast."

"Where did they come from anyway? And this other stuff, too—the pillow and the fan? I really thought I was in the wrong place when I saw them."

"Stacy bought them to make the place feel more comfortable."

"No kidding?" Roni mused, munching on a second doughnut. "Didn't you guys go out last night?"

"Yeah, but we found this great, all-night bazaar, too. Actually, some guys we met found it. They're freshmen from Penn State."

"Penn State, huh? Great! Any interesting prospects?"

"I don't think so," Terry answered.

"No one who meets our high standards" Sam teased. They all laughed.

Roni couldn't help smiling, thinking of the stories she'd told to Zack and the others the night before, about her own high standards, and the fabulous gifts her father bribed her with. Impishly, she wondered what would happen if she took Stacy's bamboo fan to the beach and told them all it had just arrived from India—the property of a maharaja or something. They'd probably believe her.

"What else did you do?" Roni asked.

"That's all. We had dinner, went to the bazaar, and came home."

"That's it?"

"It was fun," Sam protested.

"Well, I had a blast," Roni boasted. She told them all about her impromptu striptease.

"Sounds . . . er . . . great," Terry said dubiously.

"It was, really—it was, a real scream. I guess . . . uh . . . you had to be there," Roni added. "I mean, no one took it seriously or anything, so don't worry about my morals. I was completely covered at all times," she said modestly.

"I guess it does sound funny," Sam said.

"I was the hit of the evening," Roni insisted. There was a knock at the door. "Are you guys expecting anyone?"

"The vice squad," Terry quipped as she put the groceries into the tiny refrigerator at the kitchen end of the suite. Pulling back the front curtain, Sam peered out. Roni stood on tiptoes, looking over her head.

"It's them!" she shrieked. "That's Lisa in front, and the cute guy next to her is Zack, and that's Ray. Quick, Sam, get the door. I'm not dressed."

"They're your friends, you let them in. I'm going to go change into my bathing suit." Sam retreated to her room.

Roni glanced down at the long Hawthorne T-shirt she had worn to bed and shrugged. It was decent enough, she figured. As she hurried to the door, she combed her fingers through her hair, hoping it looked okay.

Lisa, outrageous in a yellow cotton coverup and bright red heels, turned toward her slowly as the door opened. She had on super-large sunglasses, and Roni sensed her eyes were only half-open behind them.

"Too much sun this early in the day." Lisa grumbled.

"Tell me about it," Roni agreed. "So, what's up?"

"A barbecue," Lisa told her, sounding a little more enthusiastic. "And an all-day volleyball tournament. I'm not playing," she added quickly. "You won't catch me jumping around like that, not with this head."

"You, too?" Roni groaned. "Mine feels like it weighs two tons."

"No kidding. We're talking major headache," Ray chimed in. "I had more to drink than the rest of you put together."

Roni groaned, afraid she might be sick if he kept

talking about it. "Did we really drink all that?" She shook her head in disbelief.

Lisa laughed. "All except Zack, our designated driver." She rolled her eyes as if she didn't think much of the idea. "Anyway, go put on your suit," she told Roni, as she turned to leave. "We'll wait in the Jeep."

"Two minutes," Roni called back. Gingerly, she pulled the door closed behind her. Even the tiniest noise seemed to jar her aching head. Making her way slowly across the room, Roni went into the bathroom and started to brush her teeth.

"So what's going on," Sam asked from the doorway.

Roni quickly rinsed her mouth and dashed water on her face. "I've got to hurry. Lisa and those guys are waiting for me."

Sam looked disappointed. "I thought you were spending the day with us?"

Roni froze, her washcloth dripping into the sink. "Oh, well . . ." she began, giving Sam an apologetic look.

"Don't tell me you forgot."

"I didn't forget," Roni insisted. "I just didn't know about this barbecue. Anyway, I already told Lisa I'd go and they're waiting for me." She bit her lip. "You guys could come along," she said without much enthusiasm. Somehow having Sam and Terry along would put a damper on her fun. She felt more comfortable on her own, without her roommates there to watch her every move. Still, she had promised. "Maybe I could meet you guys later."

"We're planning to take that long walk down the

beach later. Should I count you in?"

"I don't know. I forgot to ask when the barbecue starts."

Sam didn't say anything.

"Sam, we're here to have fun," Roni protested. "And, after all, we can take a walk anytime."

"I know." Sam turned to leave and then stopped, gazing back at Roni. "Look, we'll try to find your volleyball game, how's that? The four of us could be a team."

"I guess so," Roni said. "Listen, if we find one another, great. If not, there's always tomorrow."

That seemed to satisfy Sam. Relieved, Roni hurried to get dressed. She didn't want to keep Lisa waiting.

Roni was so stuffed with hamburgers, hot dogs, and barbecued corn on the cob that she was sure she'd never eat again.

"Guess the party's over," Lisa said, crumpling up the last empty potato chip bag. Beside her, Mary Lou and Evelyn were packing suntan lotion and magazines into their beach bags.

"A nice, hot shower and then an ice-cold drink, that's what I want," Evelyn said dreamily, smoothing back her curly blonde hair. "Our room is so far away, though."

Zack plopped down on the blanket next to her. "My room's not that far. You could shower there," he suggested.

Evelyn pretended to be shocked. "Me, use a strange man's shower? Never!"

"Yeah, he is pretty strange," Lisa teased.

Roni listened jealously. Evelyn had been flirting shamelessly with Zack all day.

"I'm too tired to bother you, if that's what you're worried about," Zack said. "That last game of three-on-three did me in."

"Last game? The tournament's over?" Roni looked up in surprise. The sun's rays were slanting low over the water. "Wow! How did it get so late?"

"Time flies when you're having fun," Evelyn said coyly. She sat close to Zack, her thigh pressing against his leg. "You're a great coach," she told him. "You really improved my serve."

"Anything to help the team," Zack said lazily.

"You looked pretty good," Roni cut in. "But if I hadn't had that awful headache all day, I could've shown you a thing or two."

"We got along just fine without you," Evelyn observed.

"I don't know," Roni insisted. "Your serve's not perfect, you know, Zack. I think you need more practice." She grabbed the volleyball. Evelyn had managed to keep Zack to herself all day, and Roni thought it was about time she got some attention.

"All I need is a good long nap," Zack said. Ignoring Roni, he stretched out flat, cradling his head in his arms.

Roni dropped the volleyball and picked a floppy khaki hat up off the blanket. "Here," she said, casually dropping it onto the side of Zack's face, "it will keep you from burning."

"Mmm. Thanks."

"You got pretty red out there today." Hesitantly, she poked his shoulder with her finger. It left a white dot, while the skin around it turned flaming. "You'd better cover yourself up," she told him, searching for an extra towel to drape over his back.

"Use some of this." Lisa tossed Roni a tube of sunblock.

"Do you mind?" she asked Zack.

"Women," he muttered. "Always fussing."

"I could just let you burn."

"Okay, okay, don't get huffy. Please, save my skin." Zack looked out from under the hat and grinned.

Evelyn shot Roni a dirty look as she squeezed a long stream of lotion onto his back and began to massage it into his shoulders. His skin was hot from hours of being in the sun.

"I'm going for a swim," Evelyn announced. "Anyone want to come?"

No one answered. She waited for a moment, then turned and ran toward the ocean.

"I'll go in, too," Lisa suddenly said. She grabbed Ray's hand and pulled him up, dragging him toward the water. Mary Lou followed them. As she watched them go, her fingers still smoothing the lotion onto Zack's smooth, warm skin, Roni felt almost embarrassed.

"I guarantee you'll have the best tan this side of the Rockies," she quipped, to hide her confusion.

Zack rolled over and caught her hands in his. His gray eyes looked at her so intently, she felt her mouth go dry. "Alone at last," he said. Roni held her breath, thinking he might kiss her. But instead he grinned and raised his eyebrows.

Roni drew her hands away and put the cap back

on the sunblock. Forcing a laugh, she said, "For a minute, I thought you were serious."

"Why would I be?" Zack studied her. "You haven't said two serious words to me yet."

"So? This is vacation."

"What are you like when you're *not* on vacation?"

Roni tossed her hair and shrugged. "I'm always the same. Aren't you?"

He studied her for a moment. "Sure. I'm always the life of the party."

"No, *I'm* the life of the party." Playfully, she pushed his shoulder.

"You confuse me. You tell all these stories about yourself, but somehow I don't feel like I know you at all."

"I don't know anything about you, either." Roni grinned slyly. "Except that you're a lousy drummer," she added.

"Hey, take that back!"

Roni leaped to her feet. "Never! You're the worst drummer I ever heard." She jumped away from the blanket, kicking sand in his direction. Wiping the sand away, he came after her.

"Can't catch me," she called. With a yelp of excitement, she turned and sprinted down the beach. Zack was right on her heels. Roni ran as fast as she could, dodging between sunbathers and couples strolling, but Zack was still gaining on her.

She veered toward the water, where the sand was wet and solid underfoot. She'd never outrun Zack, she realized as she peeked over her shoulder. He was right there. Squealing helplessly, Roni splashed into the surf. Zack grabbed for her arm and, giggling wildly, Roni threw handfuls of water into his face. Zack ducked, protesting and laughing. Holding his hands up in front of his face, he followed her deeper into the water. When he caught her, he threw his arms around her, squeezing her tight.

"Let me go!" Roni gasped.

He scooped her up in his arms. "Say please."

"Zack! No, put me down!" She squealed with delight, kicking and thrashing.

"Right here?" He lifted her higher, threatening to drop her into the deep waves.

"No!" Roni threw her arms around his neck. Her heart was pounding, as she gasped for breath. She could feel Zack's heart pounding also. His face was only inches away from hers.

"You have a scar," she said breathlessly, looking at his face more closely. "I never noticed it before. A tiny one, there, under your left eyebrow."

He caught his breath and grinned. "I know," he said quietly. For a second they just looked at each other, and then Zack's lips touched hers. Roni felt dizzy as she let him kiss her. And then, before she realized it, she was kissing him back.

Chapter 5

Water splashed over the back of Roni's head.

"Hey, you two," Evelyn interrupted. "Lisa and Ray are ready to leave."

Roni pulled her head back. "Let them," she said without even looking at Evelyn. But Zack loosened his grip and lowered Roni to her feet. She tried to steady herself as a huge wave broke over them, knocking her into Zack. If Evelyn hadn't been standing right there, it could have been a romantic moment. Roni would have thrown herself against Zack and clung to him, using the strong waves as an excuse. But Evelyn obviously wasn't going away.

"Where are they headed?" Zack wanted to know.

"Back to the bungalow," Evelyn said, looking pointedly at Roni. "I guess we all need a break—in our own rooms."

"Need a nap, Evelyn?" Roni asked, flashing the other girl a sarcastic smile. "Some of us have outgrown those."

Evelyn looked at her coldly. "No one has any plans for tonight, so we might as well get some rest from the sun."

"No plans!" Roni cried in shock. "What's the

matter with you guys? We're on spring break in
Florida! You don't need to make plans—just hit the
beach and stay there."

"Roni's right," Zack agreed. "I don't want to waste
a minute of my vacation." He splashed both hands
into the water, showering both girls with torrents of
water.

Roni shrieked and splashed him back. Evelyn
glared at Zack, angrily brushing water from her
face.

"Hey, I have an idea." Roni smiled happily at
Zack. "Let's go to the drive-in! We passed it on our
way into town—the Moonglow."

"A drive-in!" Zack's eyes lit up. "I haven't been to
one since I was a little kid."

"They're even better when you're older," Evelyn
said, gazing into Zack's eyes.

Roni stepped between them. "I thought you were
staying in tonight, Evelyn."

She shrugged. "Not if everyone else is going out."

Roni took Zack by the arm. "We can take your
Jeep," she suggested. "And Ray and Lisa can go
with Evelyn in her car."

Zack nodded. "Sounds fine with me."

Evelyn narrowed her eyes. "My car's been acting
funny today. I'd rather not drive."

"Well, we can't all go in one car," Roni pointed
out.

"I'm not taking mine, and that's final." Evelyn
said, pouting.

"Great." Roni rolled her eyes.

"Just one big happy family," Zack observed. He
splashed them again, and as they stood dripping

and gasping, he raced up the beach. "Last one to the drive-in's a wet blanket!" he yelled.

Roni sprinted after him, and Evelyn was behind her. Out of breath, Roni reached their blanket first, but Zack just ignored her. By then, everyone was packing up their stuff, ready to call it a day.

Roni pulled Lisa aside. "What's with Evelyn?"

"What do you mean?"

"Is she after Zack?"

Lisa shrugged. "How should I know?"

"Well, was she interested in him before you came down here?"

Lisa looked annoyed and rubbed her forehead. "I don't know."

"Do you know if Zack is interested in her?" Roni persisted.

"Maybe. Look, they're friends. We're all friends."

"You're no help at all." Roni stood there, her hands on her hips, facing Lisa in disgust.

"What do you want me to do?" Lisa protested. "I don't know who Zack likes. He's better friends with Steve and Mark than with me or Ray. Ask them if you're so interested."

"I'm more comfortable asking you about it," Roni admitted.

"He's a wild guy, you're a wild girl. Go for it."

"Lisa!" Roni didn't bother to hide her annoyance. "You're not taking this very seriously."

Lisa rolled her eyes. "Look who's talking about being serious. Give me a break, Roni."

Zack came over. "Lis, are you coming to the drive-in?"

"You bet." Lisa turned and examined the group. "We need more cars, though."

"No, we don't!" Roni exclaimed, getting an idea. "We'll make it a contest. We'll get everyone into Zack's car—the more the merrier. Right, Evelyn?"

"You're crazy," Evelyn told her.

Ignoring her, Roni ran up and down the beach, gathering together anyone who looked friendly. In no time she had more than a dozen people struggling to fit inside the Jeep. Lisa nearly collapsed, she was laughing so hard. Kids were climbing on one another's laps and squeezing into every available inch of space. When it looked like no more bodies could possibly fit in, Roni pulled in four more people.

"Twenty!" she called, making a final head count.

How they all fit, no one knew. Roni got in last, ignoring the squeals and yelps of pain as she climbed over a tangled pile of arms and legs.

"Where's the lemonade?" Lisa called. "Leave room for the lemonade!"

Somehow, someone managed to pass her the Thermos they'd filled with gin and lemonade, and Lisa took a long drink, then passed it on. The whole scene was so funny that Zack didn't even complain about people crowding his shifting arm. Behind them, the kids who couldn't fit into the Jeep had climbed into Ray's car, which was also stuffed. Someone even brought another car over. By that time, Roni had lost count of how many people there were.

The three cars made a noisy convoy down the beach. At the drive-in they piled out. The Moonglow was straight out of the fifties, but it was really decrepit—everything was falling apart. For a minute, Roni was almost sorry they came. Then she spotted the children's playground just to the side of the giant old movie screen.

"Hey, look! Let's play on the swings!" She ran toward them.

"Get a seesaw!" Zack yelled, running after her. "You're looking at a true seesaw champion."

"Oh, yeah?" Roni climbed on one side and Zack climbed on the other. Immediately, he bumped his end so hard against the ground that Roni thought she would fly off. She bounced up in the air and landed back on the board with a solid thump.

"Ouch! That hurt!" She glared resentfully at Zack.

"I warned you."

When she reached the ground, Roni jumped off her end, sending Zack crashing to the ground.

"Ouch!"

"You should have been ready!" Roni cried with a giggle.

Zack stood up, looking at her with a strangely serious expression. "You know, I think I'm beginning to understand you."

"What's there to understand?" Roni asked, shrugging. "It's simple, just like I told you—I have fun and I do what I want."

"That's what you say, but I think there's more to it than that," Zack replied, shaking his head.

"Don't be ridiculous."

"It's your whole background. That kind of stuff's bound to affect you."

"What are you, a psych major or something?

Don't analyze everything." Roni squirmed, a little
uncomfortable about Zack thinking so hard about
the stories she'd told him. She wasn't sure she could
remember all the details and keep them straight.
"Hey, I thought you were the guy who likes mys-
teries?"

"Only in books," he said.

Lisa appeared just then, clutching the Thermos.
She passed it to Roni. "Drink up!"

"More lemonade?" Roni took a sip and then
passed it back to Lisa. "Not much left," she said.

"Then let's get some more."

They took up a collection and sent a group to the
convenience store they'd passed on the way in.
When they came back, someone passed around a
bottle of rum and they spiked all the Cokes. Someone else put vodka in the iced tea. By then,
everyone was horsing around on the playground
equipment. Some kids were pretty drunk already.

Evelyn was pushing Mark on the swings, and Lisa
took the swing beside her. Ray swung her higher
and higher, making Lisa shriek loudly. Grabbing
her swing to get it to stop, Ray made it twist crazily.
When it was finally still, Lisa jumped off, twisting
one foot beneath her as she landed.

"Stupid shoes," she muttered, ripping off her high
heels.

"Here, have some." Mark said as he passed her a
rum-and-Coke. "You'll feel better."

Lisa juggled the shoes in her arms, taking the
cup. "Hey, you know what I've always wanted to
do?"

"What?"

"Watch." Grandly, Lisa held one shoe high in the air and began pouring her drink into it.

"Ugh!" Mark grimaced. "That's disgusting."

"You're supposed to use champagne!" Roni screamed, doubling over with laughter.

When Lisa had drained the shoe, Mark grabbed it and refilled it. "I dare anyone else to do that!" he yelled.

"How about you?" someone shouted.

"Ladies first," he said, bowing gallantly. Mark held the shoe out to Roni, and gamely, she took a sip. She made a face when she was through, though.

"Give me the other one." Mark took it and began passing the red shoes around, daring everyone to take a drink.

"Uh-oh," Roni whispered loudly. "I see a party-pooper."

A tall man in a blue uniform approached them. "There's no liquor allowed here," he warned. "Let's go."

Roni held up her cup. "You mean this? This is just Coke." She smiled innocently and the man shook his head and turned to leave. They might have gotten away with it, but just then someone giggled loudly. The cop came back, serious this time.

"You'd better leave," he said.

Ray stepped up, a challenging look on his face, but Roni grabbed his arm. "Who needs the drive-in anyway?" she declared. "Let's just move this party!"

"Not the beach again," someone groaned.

"No . . . to Zack's bungalow," Roni said, inspired.

"To the bungalow!" Zack cried.

They piled into the vehicles and took off. Soon the bungalow Zack was sharing with Mark and Ray was packed. The cassette player was turned as loud as it would go and everyone was dancing.

The noise was incredible, and the noisier it got, the more people it attracted. Complete strangers were coming in and joining the fun. It seemed as though the party would never end, and Roni was one of the diehards. Finally, though, the crowd thinned out.

"Hey, everybody, I have an idea," Roni announced loudly. "It's almost dawn. Let's have a sunrise breakfast!"

"Fantastic!" Lisa cried, draining the glass in her hand. "Why didn't I think of that? Grab the food and the booze, and let's hit the beach!"

Quickly, Roni organized people into groups. She sent six guys and girls to the all-night supermarket with orders to buy plenty of eggs and potatoes and bread. Zack and Ray volunteered as short-order cooks, and a group of people headed to the part of the beach with built-in barbecue grills.

Roni, Lisa, and Evelyn followed with fresh batches of orange juice and lemonade. They'd filled every available Thermos and empty juice bottle, and Lisa had insisted on spiking every one with vodka or gin. Now Lisa stumbled, slopping some of the juice on the ground. Laughing hysterically, she plopped onto the sand, balancing pitchers and jars.

"What's so funny?" Roni asked, but by now she was laughing too. "I think we're drunk," she told Lisa.

"I'll drink to that," Lisa said, hoisting a pitcher

and spilling most of it down her shirt.

"Gross!" Roni cried, pulling Lisa to her feet. "Come on. You've had enough."

"How can you tell?" Lisa asked indignantly.

"Because I've had enough and you've had more," Roni cracked. "Let's go, they're waiting for us."

"You mean Zack's waiting," Lisa countered, raising her eyebrows. "Roni loves Zack," she started to chant. "Roni loves Zack. Zack loves Roni."

Roni froze. "Did he tell you that? Lisa, what did he say about me?"

"Told me there's no other girl for him." She giggled wildly.

Peering cautiously at the other girl's face, Roni asked, "Did he really? Tell the truth, Lisa. I need to know."

Lisa sputtered with laughter. "I don't know. He said something, I think." She frowned comically. "Or maybe Ray did. *Somebody* did."

"This isn't funny," Roni said crossly. "How can you be so mean?"

"I'm a mean, mean girl," Lisa sang.

Roni sighed and followed her to the picnic area. What good did it do to ask Lisa a question if she couldn't believe the answer?

Not long after they got there, the breakfast picnic got under way. Zack and Ray cooked scrambled eggs and home-fried potatoes on the grills for everyone.

"A man of hidden talents!" Roni exclaimed, admiring the plateful of steaming scrambled eggs Zack handed her.

"I'm full of surprises." Zack piled some fried potatoes on her plate, too.

Mark came up. "How about some sunrise volleyball, you guys?"

"Too dark," Zack replied. "If it weren't for the streetlights, I couldn't see to cook."

Mark shrugged broadly. "We're going to give it a try anyway."

Roni started to bolt her food so she could join them. Zack noticed and looked at her curiously. "Why the hurry?" he asked.

"Volleyball," Roni mumbled in between bites. "Sounds like a blast."

"Wait ... uh ... don't play. Go sit over there, okay?" He pointed to a deserted bench in a grove of tall palm trees.

"What for?"

"Trust me," he said seriously. "Find yourself a nice, comfortable spot and wait."

"For what?" Roni asked with a giggle. "Are you teasing me?"

"You'll see." Zack waved his spatula, chasing her away. Shrugging, Roni went over and sat under the biggest palm, pulling her sweater close around her.

The air was chilly—almost too cold to be comfortable, especially compared to how hot the days were. As she sat there waiting for Zack, the sky began to lighten. A family of terns appeared, skittering over the sand, their sticklike legs going faster and faster. They looked so comical that Roni found herself smiling. She felt good, happy. The salty air was fresh and crisp, and to her surprise she didn't even mind the cold.

"Beautiful, isn't it?" Plate in hand, Zack sat down on the bench beside her. He set his plate down on his lap and leaned back. There was a dreamy look on his face. "It's kind of exciting." He colored. "I mean, it's beautiful . . . I don't know." He seemed uncomfortable suddenly.

"No, I know what you mean. It's sort of . . . thrilling." Roni frowned. "I didn't sound like I meant that, but I really do."

"I know," Zack said quietly. He continued to stare out at the ocean. For a long while they just sat there, side by side, silent. A pale light glowed low in the sky behind the horizon. Then the glow seemed to spread and a band of light appeared. Roni sat up.

"The false dawn," Zack told her. "In a while the sun will really come up. You'll see."

"Have you done this a lot—watched the dawn, I mean?"

"Sure. Haven't you?"

She shrugged. "I've stayed out till dawn lots of times, but I don't think I ever watched the sun rise. And definitely not on a beach." She took a deep breath of the damp, early morning air. "It's sort of like . . . like the whole earth is waking up."

Zack nodded solemnly. "And it happens every day—day after day, year after year. So simple and so beautiful. Look!"

The sun suddenly appeared on the horizon. It grew bigger and bigger and glowed brighter. The whole sky seemed to get light at once. *Dawn.*

Roni turned to Zack. "Thanks."

He smiled at her. "For what?"

"For making me watch this. I wouldn't have missed this for the world."

Zack gazed at her silently for a long time. "Neither would I," he said finally.

Chapter 6

There was a commotion over by the barbecue, and Roni asked, "What's all the noise?"

Shrugging, Zack sprang to his feet. "Let's go look."

Roni tossed her empty plate into a trash can, and they headed up the beach. Not far away, a bunch of people stood in a circle, shouting and clapping their hands.

Zack ran ahead of Roni. "It's a limbo contest!" he yelled back to her. "Hurry! You won't believe it."

Moments later Roni arrived, breathless. "You're right, I *don't* believe it."

In front of them Lisa was bent over backward, inching her way under a pole that was only a few feet off the ground. No one could possibly slip under it, Roni thought.

She tugged on Mary Lou's arm. "What's going on?"

Red-faced from laughing, Mary Lou had to take a deep breath before she could answer. "It's a limbo contest," she said finally, gasping. "Lisa's winning. Evelyn was ahead, but she quit." Mary Lou started laughing at that.

Roni looked at her. "What's so funny about that?"

Mary Lou shook her head helplessly. Suddenly she gagged and her face turned pale.

"You don't look too good," Roni observed. "Are you okay?" Mary Lou clapped a hand over her mouth and ran for the nearest palm tree. Roni shut her eyes and tried not to listen. Grabbing her shoulders, Zack turned her toward the limbo pole.

"Don't look and don't listen or you'll get sick, too," he instructed.

Roni shuddered. She pushed her way into the circle around Lisa and joined in the clapping. Everyone urged Lisa on as she tried to wriggle beneath the limbo pole without knocking it down.

"She's going to make it!" someone cheered.

Miraculously, Lisa had almost made it. Then she had a giggling fit and collapsed flat on her back.

"Get up!" the crowd yelled.

"Come on! You can do it!" Roni cried.

"I can't!" Lisa gasped, out of breath.

Roni bent over her, pulling one arm. "Come on, get up. You can do it."

"Never. Go 'way." Lisa's head dropped back heavily and she closed her eyes.

"At least try to get up," Roni coaxed, a little worried now.

"No! Leave me 'lone," Lisa sputtered angrily. Her head flopped to one side and she looked like she was asleep.

Roni bent over and slapped Lisa's cheeks lightly. "Lis? Lisa, wake up."

Roni spied Ray in the crowd and called out to

him. "Look, can you help me?" she cried, pointing at Lisa. "I think she passed out."

"So what else is new?" Ray shrugged.

"Forget it," someone said. "Just leave her there."

"How much did she drink, anyway?" Roni peered closely at Lisa's face.

"Who knows?" Ray shrugged.

"Well, I don't think we should leave her here. She'll catch cold."

Roni tried to lift Lisa's motionless body, but it was impossible. "Talk about a dead weight," Roni muttered. "I can't budge her." She glanced at Ray. "Let's at least get her a blanket or something."

Lisa groaned and stirred in her sleep.

"We can't just leave her here. . . ." Roni searched the beach. "Where's Zack? He'll help."

"Help what?"

Roni suddenly felt angry at Ray. Was he acting dumb deliberately? "Help get her back to the bungalow," she snapped. "Don't you even care?"

"What's the big problem? She's not going to go anywhere," Ray answered matter-of-factly.

Suddenly Roni wondered how sober Ray was. She took a deep breath. "I'm going to find Zack," she said, speaking slowly and clearly. "We're going to put Lisa in the Jeep and take her to her room. Don't leave her."

Quickly, Roni found Zack and explained the situation. He hurried back with her and together he and Ray helped get Lisa up off the sand. Half dragging and half carrying, they got her to the Jeep.

"She's going to freak when she hears she did the

limbo," Ray said. "She hates the limbo."

"She'll handle it," Roni said dryly as she got into the backseat beside Lisa and propped her up. "Too bad she's missing this gorgeous morning, though. The beach is deserted."

"Perfect for racing down the beach," Zack said, patting the Jeep fondly.

Roni scanned the flat sand—miles of it, and only birds to share it with. "Well," she said slowly, "it *is* a shame to waste it." She glanced at Zack and then at Lisa. "I guess a little ride won't bother her. We'll get her home soon, right?"

"No problem," he said in an understanding tone. He threw the Jeep into gear and took off, heading across the sand toward the water.

Roni leaned over the front seat and pounded Zack's shoulder. "What are you doing?"

"Jeep-surfing." Zack threw the Jeep into high gear, chasing the waves as they rushed up to break on the sand. Weaving in and out, they sped toward the strip of motels and bungalows at their end of the beach.

Ray hung onto his door handle as Zack made a wild loop back toward the water. "She'll be fine back there, really," he called, nodding toward Lisa.

"Oh, well," Roni called back, "like you said, she's not going anywhere."

"Look at those early birds!" Zack shouted to them, pointing out a couple splashing through the waves farther up the beach.

"They've got to be crazy." Roni gawked at them, then called, "Drive closer—let's see who they are."

"Okay." Zack swerved the Jeep so suddenly that

Ray turned pale and grabbed onto the door, moaning. Zack headed straight toward the swimmers.

Roni climbed half over the front seat, putting her hand forward to press on the horn. "Happy sunrise!" she yelled. Honking and waving, Zack drove the Jeep within a few feet of the couple.

Startled, the man stared at them, one hand resting familiarly against the girl's back. The girl stared at the Jeep in shock, then broke away from the man, her dark hair flying. Roni couldn't believe her eyes: the girl was Maddie Lerner.

"They sure looked surprised," Zack commented as they passed.

"Very surprised," Roni agreed. "And guilty . . ."

Someone landed on her bed and Roni bolted upright. "Who's there?"

"It's just me, Terry." The light snapped on and Roni saw her roommate standing over her.

Roni fell back against the pillows. "I was taking a nap, or at least trying to. Turn the light off, will you?"

Terry ignored her and sat down on the edge of the bed. "I'm surprised to see you."

Stacy peeked around the door. "Oh, Roni, it's you. I thought Terry was talking to herself."

Roni pulled up the blanket. "What are you guys doing here anyway? Why aren't you out swimming or something?"

"We have been—all day. You've been asleep for hours." Stacy turned to leave the room. "Let me know if I miss any good stories," she said to Terry.

"What did she mean by that?" Roni asked, peering at Terry, who gave her a vague look.

"Nothing. She's probably just tired. We just got back from our walk down the beach." Changing the subject, she added, "Maddie came with us—we bumped into her, and she was all alone, so we asked her to join us. She's really a nice person."

Roni grinned. "Not considering what I saw." She told Terry how she'd seen Maddie with her older man, up at dawn to steal some time together. "Unless, of course, they were together all night," she finished dramatically.

"I don't believe it," Terry whispered dumbfounded. "She seems so sweet and nice with us. Not at all like someone who would . . ."

Roni shrugged. "These days, I'd believe anything. I'll bet he's one of her professors. After all, where else would she meet a guy that old. I bet he even followed her down here."

Terry gasped. "Wait, you may be right. She still wouldn't say who she was here with, but when she let slip something about 'the professor,' you should have seen her blush!"

"People can really fool you, can't they?" Roni commented.

"I guess so." Terry peeled off her swimsuit and threw on a terry-cloth robe. "I think I'm going to take a nap, too. I may not have been up as late as you were, but, boy, am I tired."

"I was up *all night*," Roni corrected her. "I just need a little more sleep, though, and then a shower before tonight's barbecue. Zack's going to be head chef."

"Really?" Terry stretched out on her bed.

Roni chuckled. "Yeah. He's great."

Terry smiled. "Sounds like you're pretty interested in him."

"I might be," Roni admitted.

"That's great, I guess."

"What do you mean, you guess?"

"Nothing," Terry said quickly. "I mean, I'm sure he's probably a nice guy."

"Sure he is." Roni shrugged. "Where's Sam, anyway?"

"We left her on the beach with Maddie."

Roni yawned. "It seems like I haven't seen Sam in ages."

Terry gaped at her. "You haven't seen any of us."

"Haven't I?"

"Not really. You know, it would have been nice if you'd come along today like you promised."

Roni groaned. "Give me a break! We don't always have to do everything together, you know. Don't make me feel guilty because I've met lots of new people and you haven't."

"But, I thought we all—"

"Terry," Roni interrupted. "I am having possibly the best time of my entire life! We can take another walk down the beach, okay? Anytime you say."

"You mean anytime you can't get a better offer."

"That's not fair," Roni said.

Terry played with the belt of her robe. "Isn't it? It seems like you do things with us only if you don't have a better offer. And you always have a better offer."

"That's not true at all! What about my Friday night parties at school? They're always in our suite.

I don't go looking for better offers then, do I?"

"No, you don't," Terry said loyally. "But at school, upperclassmen won't give you the time of day. Here they do, so you ignore us."

"Don't be this way," Roni pleaded. "I'm not trying to hurt anyone's feelings. I can't help it if I think of great things to do and Lisa's crowd wants to do them. Besides—and be honest—would you have stayed up all night for my sunrise breakfast?"

"Maybe if you'd asked," Terry said. "Look, forget it, okay? We have great plans for tonight. Why don't you come with us?"

"What are you going to do?"

"Why can't you just say yes first?" Terry demanded angrily.

"I have a right to ask, don't I?"

Terry sighed and sat on the bed next to Roni. "We're going to this great Hawaiian-style place that serves a whole stuffed pig on a spit. It's supposed to be wild: fire-eaters, hula dancers, everything!"

"That sounds terrific," Roni agreed. "I'd love to do that. Could I ask Zack to be my date?"

"None of us are bringing dates," Terry said, hesitating.

"I know, I could invite everyone in their crowd. Maybe you'll even like one of Zack's friends. Steve and Mark aren't going out with anyone."

"But now it's a whole party."

"I give up." Roni threw her hands in the air. "I don't know what you want."

"I'm sorry," Terry said soothingly. "It's not a bad idea, really—to get all our friends together. Why don't you call and ask them?"

Leaping from the bed, Roni went to the telephone in the living room. Now that she thought about it, she wasn't sure Lisa and the others would like her idea. Sure, they accepted her, but what about a whole bunch of freshmen girls? But she had to call now. Reluctantly, she dialed the phone.

Lisa answered on the fifth ring, her voice groggy.

"You sound awful," Roni told her. "Asleep, huh? I just woke up, too."

"I feel awful," Lisa groaned.

"But it was worth it, wasn't it? Last night was a blast." Roni snuggled back into the couch, ready for a long talk about everything that had happened. "The drive-in was a panic."

"Yeah, that was pretty cool," Lisa agreed.

"I could have killed Zack, bouncing me up and down on that seesaw. But my favorite was the picnic breakfast. And the sunrise was gorgeous," she added.

"Sunrise?" Lisa asked vaguely.

"Yeah, didn't you see it? It was only the most spectacular thing I've ever seen."

"I don't remember any sunrise. Are you sure you're not making this up?"

"Lisa, I was right there. So was Zack—just the two of us. We watched it forever."

"Sounds like you two really hit it off."

"I think so. I wasn't sure he liked me before, but now I'm pretty sure he does."

"Great!"

Roni chortled. "You sure looked like you had a fun time. How's the limbo champ, anyway?"

"The what?"

"Limbo champ. Ray said you wouldn't like it getting out, but your secret's safe with me."

"You're nuts!" Lisa answered. "Who made this up? Ray?"

"Lisa, don't you remember the limbo contest? You were hysterical."

"Cut it out, Roni. It's not fair to tease a hung-over person."

"You must be hung over if you forgot doing the limbo." Roni paused, then added, "Actually, it was right before you passed out."

"I didn't pass out," Lisa said crankily.

Roni held the phone away from her ear, staring at it in disbelief. "Yes, you did. No offense, but you weigh a ton. I always heard people were heavier unconscious, but I never believed it until now."

"You're making all this up," Lisa said, sounding really annoyed.

"Have it your way," Roni said finally. "Anyway, I had a fantastic time."

"Right," Lisa said, as if dismissing the subject. "So listen to what's on the agenda for tonight—"

Roni interrupted her. "Wait, I have a better idea." She described the Hawaiian restaurant, trying to make it sound really great. "How about it? Think you and Zack and Ray and the others can make The Pig Hut?"

"Roni, listen to me for a minute. We're invited to a big party . . . on a yacht!"

Terry and Stacy were talking quietly in the bedroom when Roni entered a minute later. Terry looked up expectantly.

"I heard you talking to Lisa. Is it definite for

tonight? We're really excited about meeting your new friends."

Roni squirmed uncomfortably. "Uh . . . listen, you guys—"

Stacy jumped up. "Oh, no! You didn't make other plans, did you, Roni?"

"I couldn't help it," she said, giving them a pleading look. "Lisa already made plans that included me."

"I don't believe this," Terry said, her shoulders sagging. Stacy just looked coldly at Roni.

"It really is for something special," Roni insisted. "A catered party on a yacht!"

Stacy marched for the door. "Do what you want. I don't really care anymore."

Roni turned to Terry. "Terry, I promise to spend the whole day with you guys tomorrow, honest. I can't help it about tonight—Lisa went to a lot of trouble to get me invited to this."

Terry stood up. "Oh, Roni, it isn't anyone's fault. Like you said, we're here to have fun. I guess you just know how to have more fun than the rest of us."

"You're the best roommate ever." Roni leaped onto the bed and threw her arms around Terry. "Thanks for understanding, really."

Chapter 7

The late-morning sun was weak as Roni plopped down on the beach blanket next to Stacy, letting out a deep sigh. "I never thought I'd say this, but I wouldn't mind sleeping all day."

Stacy looked up from her fashion magazine. "What? No big party today? No wild rides through the surf? No getting kicked out of drive-ins?" She reached for the suntan lotion and smoothed it over her slender arms. With her light tan and the dramatic streaks of white in her blonde hair, her aristocratic good looks were even more striking. "Don't tell me you're finally partied out."

"Maybe." Roni stretched out, digging her toes into the warm sand. "Last night's party may have topped my list of all-time greats."

Sam looked at her with interest. "That good, huh?"

Stacy snorted in disgust. "Big deal—a catered party. I've been to a million of those. It usually means dried-out hors d'oeuvres and gloppy sauces."

"Not this party," Roni corrected her. "This party

meant trays of stuffed shrimp and lobster, brandy mousse, exotic fruit and all the champagne you could drink."

"Lobster and brandy mousse." Sam licked her lips. "Sounds delicious."

"It was," Roni said dreamily. "Not to mention the fact that the yacht was absolutely fantastic."

Terry was clearly impressed. "What did it look like? Who was there—anyone famous? Was it formal?"

"Hardly." Roni laughed. "I wore my turquoise mini-dress, but lots of people were just wearing bathing suits and coverups. Zack had on jeans and he fit in just fine."

Stacy yawned and rolled onto her back. "Why did I plaster myself with this sunscreen? Now there's no sun!"

Looking up, Roni noticed the sky had suddenly clouded over. "Oh no! Now what will we do?"

"A cloudy day's better for sleeping, anyway," Stacy muttered. "I thought that's what you wanted to do."

Rolling over, Roni pounded a hollow into the sand under the blanket and fluffed up her beach towel as a pillow under her head. She closed her eyes, but she couldn't get comfortable.

Roni glanced over at her roommates. Stacy was absorbed in her fashion magazines, and Terry was scouring a newspaper, of all things—as if anything was going on in the outside world that could possibly be important to them. But Sam was the worst. She was rereading the letter she'd gotten from Aaron.

Roni could hardly hide her impatience. Here she was, spending a day with her roommates just as she'd promised, and they were all interested in other things. Meanwhile, Lisa and Zack were probably having a great time.

Finally Roni gave up trying to sleep. "Look, you guys," she said, "no offense, but this is a lousy beach day and I'm bored out of my mind. Isn't there anything to do?"

Sam looked up in surprise. "I'm not bored at all. And anyway, I really want to write Aaron a letter."

Without looking up, Stacy waved a copy of *Vogue* in Roni's face. "You can look at this if you want. There's some great **fall** sweaters."

Roni rolled her eyes. "Who wants to look at **wool** in Florida? Look, if you can't think of anything better to do, I'm going to find Lisa. I mean, I tried to hang out with you, right?"

Sam and Stacy exchanged glances. Finally Stacy gave in. "Go ahead, if you want to. Don't forget to write."

"Great! See you guys later, I promise."

But it was Friday night before Roni finally got together with her roommates.

"I can't believe tonight is my 'farewell dinner,'" Terry said mournfully as she looked into the bathroom mirror. Roni was working on Terry's makeup, giving her a dazzling new look for their last night in Daytona. "Or that you're coming with us tonight," she added. "I was beginning to think we'd never see you again."

Roni paused, waving her makeup brush in the air.

"The time just flew," she said sheepishly. "I can't believe it's our last night either. I really meant to spend more time with you."

"Well, at least we'll be together tonight." Terry drew in a deep breath.

"Worried about your new job, huh?" Roni asked, eager to change the subject.

"I'm excited about everything and all," Terry confessed, "but I still can't imagine not being back at school with you guys."

"I know what you mean," Roni told her. "This vacation seemed to go so fast."

"Not just that," Terry said, turning her head and making Roni smudge her eye shadow terribly. "On Monday, you'll be back in classes—but I'll be heading for work." Under the carefully applied makeup, Terry paled and took a deep breath. "I hope I'm doing the right thing."

"There's only one way to find out," Roni said easily, "so stop second-guessing yourself. Take a tip from me: take each day as it comes. You'll be great at your job, and with Rob nearby, you won't be lonely. Besides, if you ever miss us, you can come visit. You're only fifty miles away."

"Roni's right," Sam assured Terry from the doorway. "This is a great move for you."

"There, that is the face of success." Roni corrected the eye shadow and turned Terry toward the light.

Terry stared at herself. "I can't believe it's me," she said softly. Roni's expert makeup job brought out the best in Terry's features. The most startling change was her hair. Roni had painstakingly woven together tiny strands while Terry's hair was wet. It had dried naturally all afternoon—Terry protected it under a shower cap when she took her shower.

Now Roni carefully untwisted each braid, fluffing the rippling strands with a pick. Terry's hair stood out full and glamorous, with sun-bleached highlights.

"You look gorgeous," Stacy told her.

The fantastic makeup job and extravagant hairdo weren't the only changes in Terry. Her sunburn had finally turned a deep, golden tan, and on a whim, Terry had splurged on a fabulous sleeveless turtleneck knit dress that clung to every curve. Or, as Roni put it, it showed curves Terry didn't even know she had.

"You look like a famous TV star," Stacy said thoughtfully. She glanced down at her own dress, a pale rose linen sheath that was beautiful in its simplicity. "Maybe I'd better change," she said, completely serious. "No one's even going to notice me with Terry around."

"Not if I can help it," Roni joked. "Actually," she added, inspecting Terry at arm's length, "Terry deserves the spotlight tonight. And besides, I don't think any of us could steal it from her if we tried. She looks too incredible."

Terry whirled in a circle. "I feel incredible. Now if our evening lives up to the way we look . . ."

Roni chuckled. "Stick with me, kid, and do everything I do."

"I'm not that crazy," Terry quipped.

"Okay, then just be yourself," she said with a smile.

Sam reminded them that their reservation was for eight o'clock, so they'd better hurry. They were going to Chez Felice, a tiny French restaurant that was supposed to have the best food around.

"Wait," Roni told them all as they were getting ready to go. "Time for a final inspection. I want to make sure we all look fabulous."

"Are you kidding?" Sam teased. "People will be asking who these four gorgeous women are."

"They'll probably think we're all models or movie stars," Terry added gaily.

"We could be," Roni assured them. Everyone was giggling and laughing as they locked the motel room door behind them.

In the car, Terry squeezed Roni's arm. "It's fun to have you here," she whispered. "You can really put excitement in an evening."

"Thanks." Surprised and pleased, Roni squeezed her roommate's arm and sat back to enjoy the pleasant drive.

Chez Felice was decorated tastefully, with fine linens and fresh flowers at every table.

"Let's have a long, leisurely meal," Terry said as they took their seats.

"You don't want tomorrow to come, do you?" Sam asked, leaning over to take Terry's hand.

"Hey, this is a celebration," Roni chided. "Let's just make sure Terry has a night to remember."

"Agreed," Sam and Stacy said together.

"Fine. Waiter . . . a bottle of champagne here, please," Roni ordered. "And I'll have a rum-and-tonic to start."

"That's a lot to drink," Terry observed, trying to sound casual.

"We'll need it," Roni answered, "for all the toasts we have to make. First of all," she said, lifting her water glass, "here's to Terry's new job." She took a sip and nearly choked.

Sam leaped up. "What's wrong?"

Roni sputtered, pulling Sam back down. "Over there," she muttered, pointing across the room.

"What?" Sam craned her neck to see.

"It's Maddie—with that man," Roni said.

Terry turned to look and Sam yanked her arm. Sam bent her head low over the table, stealing glances at Maddie's companion. "Don't act so obvious. They'll see us watching."

"He is nice-looking," Stacy murmured, "for an older man, that is."

"What does she see in someone that old?" Terry's face was scarlet.

"Don't sound so shocked," Stacy told her. "It happens all the time."

"Not to anyone I know," Terry murmured.

Roni stood up. "I want to get a closer look," she said. "I'm going to go find out what's going on."

Sam grabbed her arm. "Don't you dare embarrass Maddie."

"I'll be discreet," Roni swore.

"Fat chance," Sam murmured. "Look!" she gasped, her eyes widening in shock. "A woman is joining them."

Roni gawked. "It's the same woman I saw at the beach. I don't get it."

The woman sat down at the table and the three

of them—Maddie, the man, and the woman—chatted comfortably. Then Maddie threw back her head, laughing.

By now Terry, Stacy, and Sam were staring openly. Roni lifted a hand and gave a gay little wave, giggling. "Come on. Let's find out what's happening."

"For goodness sake, Roni!" Sam hissed at her. But the damage was done—Maddie had already seen her. Maddie's face turned almost as red as Terry's. She said a few words to her two companions, excusing herself.

"She's coming over here." Terry slunk down in her chair. "I don't believe it."

"I don't know if I'm more embarrassed for us or for Maddie," Sam admitted.

Resolutely, Maddie marched to their table and planted herself at Sam's side. "Hi."

"Oh, hi," Sam answered, trying to sound unconcerned.

"Having a good time?" Roni asked. Sam elbowed her rudely. "What's wrong," Roni grumbled. "She knows we saw her. Who's the guy, Maddie?"

Stacy put a hand over her eyes, shaking her head in disbelief. "Cool it, Roni."

"Are you kidding? The three of them, together?" Roni pulled an empty chair from the next table, motioning for Maddie to sit down. "Tell us all about it."

Squirming, Maddie sat on the edge of the chair. "You . . . know about it already?"

Stacy folded her hands together primly. "You don't have to explain. It's none of our business."

"I'd like to. I . . . I think I'd feel better if I finally admit it."

"You will," Roni said, nodding encouragingly. "Tell us everything."

"Roni, stop it." Sam reached over and squeezed Maddie's hand, then quickly pulled her own hand away. "Stacy's right, it's not our business. Whatever"—she colored—"arrangements you have are completely personal."

Maddie struggled for words. "I'm so embarrassed," she whispered.

"I should think so!" Roni cried, ignoring Sam's efforts to quiet her down. "It was one thing for you to fool around with the guy, but the three of you together? That's awful."

Terry put her hands over her ears. "Enough! I don't want to hear this."

Roni glared at her. "Grow up, Terry. Let's hear the sordid details," she added, turning eagerly to Maddie. "Did he follow you down here? What about his wife—how did she find you?"

Maddie looked puzzled. "We came together, of course."

Roni gaped. "You weren't trying to keep it a secret?"

Terry, feeling the agony of Maddie's confession, pushed her chair back to leave the table. "I really don't want to hear about it."

Maddie stared at her. "Huh? I don't understand. I mean, sure—I'm embarrassed to be here with my parents, but why should you guys . . ."

Sam nearly jumped across the table. "Your *parents?*" she shrieked.

Maddie looked mystified. "What did you think? I mean, everyone else is here with friends, and, well, I know it's silly, but I felt like such a baby. . . ."

Stacy burst out laughing. "Your parents! We thought . . ." She choked on her words and couldn't go on.

"You thought what?" Maddie turned to Sam, who sputtered helplessly.

"Well, we thought"—she took a deep breath and said it all at once—"we thought you were having an affair with a married man."

Maddie gaped at her.

"You were so secretive," Sam continued solemnly. "We knew something wasn't right. And then Roni saw your parents"—Sam began to grin—"having a big fight on the beach. . . ."

"Right," Roni jumped in. "Your mom stomped off, furious."

Maddie started laughing quietly. "My mom and dad are both English professors. They were arguing about some dates, and Mom ran back to the room for a textbook."

"Oh. Well, anyway, then you came by," Roni said, "and I saw him flirt with you." She paused, shaking her head. "At least it looked that way to me."

"We were talking, not flirting." Maddie started to laugh and couldn't stop. "I can't believe . . . you thought I was his . . . girlfriend."

"He's pretty good-looking," Roni said, defending herself.

Sam and Terry hooted out loud. Everyone except Roni laughed uproariously.

Stacy sat back, looking smugly satisfied. "I swear,

Roni, you have too much imagination for one person."

"Hey, you all thought so!" Roni cried.

"That's true," Sam admitted between laughs. "It seemed to make sense. And I was"—she gasped for air—"so upset because you seemed . . . too nice to be a home-wrecker." She and Maddie exploded into fresh gales of laughter.

Roni finished off her drink. "Don't blame me," she said. "I only know how it looked." She made a face. "Ugh! Imagine being down here with your parents. Poor Maddie," she said, giving the girl a sympathetic look.

Maddie wiped a tear from her cheek, still laughing. "Actually, they're great people."

Roni laughed. "Parents, great people? That's impossible!"

"They really are," Maddie insisted. "They're both lots of fun, and really interesting. I shouldn't have been at all embarrassed about them."

"Did they teach at your old school?" Stacy asked.

"Yes, at Northwestern University. I spent my first quarter there before I realized that I wanted to go a little farther away from home."

"I understand." Roni nodded knowingly. "It's bad enough going to college in your hometown, but having your parents right on campus! Forget it!"

"That's why I transferred," Maddie admitted, "but don't hold it against them. I'd really like you to meet them."

"No way," Roni said curtly. "I came here to get away from parents."

Sam gave Maddie an apologetic look. "Don't be

offended, Maddie. I think Roni's had a bit too much to drink," she added quietly.

"Where do you live on campus?" Terry asked quickly.

"Actually, I live with my aunt off campus—about forty minutes away."

"An aunt is almost as bad as parents," Roni said.

Maddie smiled pleasantly. "I didn't have any choice. There weren't any dorm rooms available in the middle of the semester."

Roni shook her head. "Imagine, living with your aunt and spending spring break with your parents. You must be going crazy."

Sam put an arm around Maddie's shoulders. "She got to spend time with us. That was fun."

"Big deal." Roni waved her empty cocktail glass. "I've spent vacations with my family, so believe me, I know what it's like. Nothing but rules, rules, rules. They had more rules for vacations than when we were at home."

The others exchanged uncomfortable glances.

"Maybe they were trying to make sure you didn't get hurt." Terry said, sounding as practical as ever.

Roni scoffed. "Not my parents. I'm sure they just wanted to make me miserable. You don't know them. All they care about is what their precious friends think—or their business associates, or the members at the club. Always other people. They never cared about me."

Terry frowned. "I can't believe that, Roni. Maybe they were strict, but I'm sure they love you."

Roni looked at Stacy for support. "Tell her, Stacy. Tell her what it's like to be a poor little rich girl."

"I never had that problem," Stacy said quietly. "My folks were never around."

"You were lucky," Roni insisted. "Mine were always there, terrified I'd do something to attract the wrong kind of attention. 'Don't rock the boat,' they said. Both of them expected me to be a perfect little princess, a little statue."

Stacy grinned wryly. "You must have been quite a shock to them."

"You bet I was," Roni said proudly. "And why not? They deserved a little shaking up."

"Even if they did," Terry cut in, "sometimes you have to think about other people's feelings."

"I *do*," Roni protested, a hurt expression on her face. "I'm a good roommate, aren't I? I'm there when you need me."

Stacy let out a hoot.

Roni turned to her, offended. "What's that supposed to mean?"

Stacy raised her eyebrows, and Sam and Terry exchanged a meaningful glance.

"You can let people down in lots of ways," Maddie said softly.

Roni stared and Maddie looked uncomfortable.

Quickly, Sam changed the subject. "Now that Maddie's in the clear, Roni's the only person who found herself a boyfriend down here."

"Zack," Roni announced proudly.

"Zack?" Maddie repeated in a curious voice.

Roni nodded. "Zack Cooper. He's from Hawthorne, believe it or not."

"Wait a minute," Maddie said thoughtfully,

"There's a boy named Zack Cooper in my creative writing class. It's not him, is it?"

"If he's a junior, that's probably him," Roni said boastfully.

"Wait. You have classes with a junior?" Sam asked Maddie.

She shrugged. "I had advanced-placement credits from high school—honors English. But anyway, it's a terrific class, and Zack is one of the best writers. He's always asked to read his things out loud. He's very talented."

Roni frowned at Maddie. "Zack? A writer? Nah, must be another Zack Cooper."

"It's not a very common name," Terry pointed out.

Roni frowned. "I don't think he's the creative type. He just likes to party."

Stacy eyed her coolly. "You've spent practically all day with him, every day since we got here. Don't you ever talk to each other?"

"Of course we do," Roni snapped, offended. She ran a hand through her hair. "All the time."

"What do you talk about?" Maddie asked, leaning closer to Roni. "I'm curious."

"I think someone has a crush on Zack Cooper," Stacy teased.

Maddie shook her head. "No, I really don't. It just doesn't sound like he's the same guy as the Zack in my class. That Zack is a real hard worker."

Roni shrugged. "I don't know, I guess it could be the same guy. We never talked about school."

"But you don't really know anything about him," Stacy said.

Terry cut her off, trying to smooth things over. "I think it's exciting that he's a good writer. I really admire creative people."

"Maybe he's your type, then," Stacy commented acidly.

Roni stiffened. "I'm creative, too."

"Don't get huffy," Stacy told her. "I just meant that he and Terry are both hard workers. Face it, Roni, you only work hard at partying."

"That's just the way Zack likes me." Roni tossed her head defiantly.

Stacy shrugged. "You know best."

"I do." She gave Maddie a meaningful look and Maddie stood up, clearly uncomfortable. "I'd better get back to my table. My ... uh ... 'boyfriend' is waiting," she said with a giggle.

"That sure was a good one." Roni guffawed. "Hey, this bottle's empty!" she cried, shaking the champagne. "Waiter! Another bottle here."

"None for me," Terry said.

"Me either," Stacy and Sam agreed.

"Well, I want more. Where's that waiter?" she called impatiently.

"Maybe you've had enough to drink," Sam suggested quietly.

"Not me." Roni hoisted her empty champagne glass. "I want to toast everyone in this wonderful restaurant!"

"Roni," Sam whispered, smiling, "lower your voice. People are staring."

"So?" Roni was feeling good and she wanted to share her bubbly mood. "This is a wonderful restaurant, and I love everyone here."

Across the table, Stacy grinned wryly. "You'd like anyone after drinking as much as you have."

Not only was Stacy being a pain, she was acting ridiculously naïve. She was practically raised on wine and champagne.

"You call this drinking?" Roni cried. "We split that bottle four ways. I'll bet Lisa could polish it off herself."

"Now there's something to brag about," Stacy said sarcastically.

"Nobody asked you," Roni snapped. "Just remember you guys begged me to spend time with you." As if this evening was all her idea! Roni could have spent this last night with Lisa—having fun.

Sam smiled brightly. "No more squabbling. This is Terry's big night."

"Right," Roni declared, "so we should have more fun. Sam, your glass is nearly empty."

"I have plenty," Sam said quickly, holding her hand over the glass.

Roni groaned. "What's the matter with you guys? Don't you know how to party? Loosen up! Do what I do!"

"This is a fine party just the way it is," Terry said emphatically. "I love it. Really, and I'm glad we're all together."

"Hey, it's time for dessert," Sam declared. "How about chocolate mousse? You'll love it, Roni."

Roni shook her head. "Not for me." She craned her neck and signaled the waiter. "But maybe some more champagne . . ."

"Coffee sounds good," Sam suggested.

"Doesn't it," Terry immediately agreed. Roni

threw up her hands. There was no hope! The waiter arrived. "Black coffee all around," Terry ordered before Roni could say anything.

"Margarita," Roni interrupted. "What are we doing next?" she asked as soon as he had gone.

Terry checked her watch. "It's pretty late. Maybe we should get back to the room."

"You're missing the point." Roni leaned toward her. "I want to celebrate!"

Sam exchanged looks with Terry. "We do have to check out early in the morning. I wouldn't mind packing tonight."

"That's a great way to party," Roni sneered. Where was the waiter when she needed him? No wonder this party was dying.

"Listen to Sam," Terry teased, glancing nervously at Roni. "Can't wait to get back to Aaron." She took a deep breath. "I'm a little anxious, too," she added. "As soon as we get back, I have to fix up my new apartment."

"I can't believe you guys!" Roni cried. She turned to Stacy. "You're not ready to leave, are you, Stacy? You can't let that gorgeous dress go to waste. The night is young!" Roni waited for a reaction. Surely Stacy couldn't resist a party.

Just then, the waiter brought their coffee, leaving the bill at the same time. Stacy picked up a cup and sipped. "What do you want, Roni—another beer bash? Haven't you had enough of those to last a lifetime? Look," she added, her tone softer now. "I had some fun, got a fabulous tan, and got a break from school. That's what I came here for, but now it's over."

Roni looked at them all in disgust. "Well, I want more. You guys are a bunch of old ladies!" Shakily, she pushed her chair back and stood beside the table. Her voice rose. "Party-poopers," she called them. "If that's how you're going to be, I'll just have to have fun without you."

Standing beside her chair, Roni wavered unsteadily. Sam sprang up, gripping Roni's arm firmly. "Sit down and we'll talk about it," she urged quietly. Terry flushed, glancing around the restaurant, embarrassed at the scene they were making. Stacy simply looked bored.

Roni pulled her arm out of Sam's grasp, "But I look good tonight," she complained loudly. "Too good to waste myself on you ... you party-poopers."

Stacy's eyes opened wide. "You think you look good? Do you think staggering around is attractive?"

"Who's staggering?" Roni asked as she turned toward Stacy, losing her balance slightly. Reaching for a chair with which to steady herself, she knocked into the next table. The couple sitting there gasped as their table tottered. Their glasses clinked loudly and the crystal vase in the center of the table threatened to fall.

Roni colored. "Oops!—Sorry," she said, straightening the vase. The couple stared at her, incredulous.

"I don't believe this," Stacy muttered.

Roni turned in confusion. She had meant to do something—what was it?

Terry looked as if she was going to cry. Cheeks

flaming, Sam grabbed for Roni's arms and tried to turn her back to their table, but Roni pulled away.

"Please, Roni, sit down with us and have coffee. We're worried about you."

Roni grabbed her purse. "Forget it. I'm going to find Zack and Lisa. At least they know how to party." *Let them worry*! Roni thought. They were acting like a bunch of uptight losers. Like a bunch of old ladies, for crying out loud!

"You don't know where Zack and Lisa are," Sam pointed out gently. "You said so yourself, earlier. Remember?"

"Is that what's upset you—that you don't know where Zack is?" Terry asked. "Oh, poor Roni."

"Don't 'poor Roni' me!" She tossed her head. "I'm not the one you should be feeling sorry for. You should feel sorry for yourselves. And for your information, Lisa didn't forget to call. She probably just called when I... was in the shower, or something."

"Fine," Stacy said. "If that's what you want to think, who am I to say anything?"

Roni faced Stacy stonily. "What do you mean? You keep saying things like that."

"Stacy..." Sam began warningly, "maybe you should keep out of this."

"No," Roni declared. "Let's hear what she has to say. I'm interested. She's been jealous of Lisa this whole vacation, and I'd like to know why."

"I'm not jealous," Stacy insisted. "I'm concerned."

"About what—me?" Roni waited impatiently, tapping her fingers on the tabletop. "Well?"

"She's concerned about you," Sam said finally.

"That's right," Stacy admitted quietly. "I—"

"Hah! That's a good one! The gorgeous, wealthy, sophisticated Stacy Swanson is worried about poor little me. I really believe that," she added sarcastically.

"Believe it," Stacy said flatly. She was obviously trying to control her temper, although Roni couldn't see what she had to be angry about. *She* was the one whose evening was on the verge of being ruined.

"This whole year," Stacy began. "Well . . . I feel like there's something among all of us, like we're real friends. And it hurts me to see a friend hang out with a person like Lisa."

"A person like Lisa?" Roni's voice rose indignantly and people started looking at them again. "Lisa is terrific! She's probably the best friend I've got."

Sam and Terry seemed stung by the remark, but Stacy hardly flinched. "She's your best friend? Come on. Everything's a joke to her! Does she take anything seriously?"

"Some people can be *too* serious," Roni declared hotly.

"Wait and see how she treats you back at school," Stacy warned.

"Lisa will treat me fine. She's not the one I'm worried about." She looked pointedly at all three of them.

Terry pushed her coffee cup at Roni. "Drink this, you'll feel better," she said kindly. "Really."

Defiantly, Roni grabbed the coffee and dumped Sam's half-finished glass of champagne into it. She gulped most of it down. It tasted horrible, but she forced herself to finish it. "One for the road," she announced. Springing up, she swept one arm around her with a dramatic flourish. "A fond farewell, my friends. I'll find another party—there's always one last party."

Looking worried now, Stacy rose from her chair. "Where do you think you're going?"

"Someplace fun!" Roni cried.

Sam sighed. "Let her go," she said at last. "We can't force her to stay with us."

Roni smiled in delight. "That's right. You can't force me to do anything. That's the way it's always been. Nobody forces me to do a thing." She marched unsteadily toward the door.

Behind her, she heard three chairs scraping against the floor as Sam, Terry, and Stacy quickly tossed some money on the table and gathered their things together.

"Hey!" Roni cried when they got to the lobby. "Are you coming with me? Great! We'll have a blast!"

She went ahead of them as they walked back to Stacy's parked car. They all piled in.

"Let me drive," Roni said, settling herself behind the wheel.

"No way!" Stacy cried. "You'd wreck my car." She pushed Roni over to the passenger's side.

"I'm in complete control," Roni swore earnestly.

"Hardly," Stacy retorted.

Terry leaned forward. "Drunk driving is a serious problem."

Roni rolled her eyes. "Thanks for the reminder, Miss Goody-Goody."

Terry blushed. "You could lose your license, and you'd have it on your record."

Roni looked at her in disgust. "Fine. I won't drive, then. Who cares? Just drop me at Lisa's." She folded her arms and didn't say another word until they reached the rented bungalow. "Thanks for the ride," she called as she leaped out of the car and slammed the door, bounding up the short walk to the front door.

Lisa answered her knock immediately. Behind her, Roni heard Stacy's car pull away.

"Roni! Come on in!" Lisa cried, obviously glad to see her. Inside, the tiny living room was dark. Roni switched on the lights and noticed a bottle of wine and several glasses on the dented coffee table.

"Where is everyone?"

Lisa sat down on the couch and refilled her wineglass. "Zack's not here, if that's what you mean. He drove back to Hawthorne this afternoon with Mary Lou, Mark, and Steve. They decided to get a jump on the traffic. Didn't he call you?"

"No." Roni's shoulders sagged with disappointment. "What about you and Ray?" she asked Lisa. "When are you guys leaving?"

"In the morning." She frowned. "What are you doing here, anyway? I thought you went out with your roommates."

"They're such a drag," Roni complained. "They went home already, but I still want to party.—After all, it is our last chance."

Lisa sipped her wine thoughtfully. "Hey, I've got a

great idea! Why don't we go get your stuff and bring it over here? We could party all night and you could sleep over here. You could drive back tomorrow with us."

Roni's eyes lit up. "Great!" She wanted to ask Lisa more about Zack, about why he hadn't called, but she couldn't. Instead, she commented casually, "Tonight won't be half as much fun without Zack and the others."

Lisa shrugged. "Easy come, easy go. We'll have a blast anyway."

"Sure. Who needs him, anyway?" Roni smiled boldly.

Chapter 8

Bored, Roni peered out the window of her art history classroom. The days definitely seemed to be getting longer, she thought, noticing that it was still light out, even though it was the last class of the day. She sighed and forced herself to pay attention. It would happen that today's class would finish late—too late to meet anyone for dinner in the dining hall. She decided to grab a quick sandwich in the commons, and maybe even stay there to get some reading done. She'd been having a hard time concentrating on her classes ever since they got back from Daytona. She could stand to do some catching up.

Since they'd been back, Roni had gotten into the habit of dropping by Lisa's room every night after dinner. Lisa usually talked her into having a glass of the special sherry she kept in her desk before they headed over to the library together. Roni always meant to study after that, but in spite of her good intentions, she rarely did. She and Lisa just had too much fun. And there was always a bunch of kids in the library who were more interested in having fun than studying. Lisa seemed to attract them all.

But at least Stacy had been wrong about one thing—Lisa was friendlier to Roni than ever. Their drive back to Hawthorne from Daytona seemed to make their friendship even stronger.

Roni had just propped her notebooks in front of her, a soda at her side, when Lisa entered the commons and headed straight for her table. She shoved her things aside and Lisa dropped her pile of books on the table and sat down, her expression tightly controlled.

"You look weird," Roni commented. "Anything wrong?"

Lisa folded her arms across her chest. She eyed Roni critically. "Something very interesting just happened," she said slowly.

"What?" Roni asked, leaning closer. She'd never seen Lisa look so serious.

"Evelyn just introduced me to one of your roommates: Stacy Swanson."

"Did she?"

"She had some . . . er . . . surprising things to say."

"No kidding." Roni started to smile, but just then a warning bell went off in her head. "Uh . . . Lisa," she said carefully, "exactly what did you and Stacy talk about?"

"Oh, nothing much," Lisa said lightly. "I happened to mention your father—the alcoholic senator—and somehow the tragic death of your brother came up, too. We had quite a chat."

Roni had almost forgotten all the wild stories she'd told Lisa in Daytona. How could she ever have been so dumb? Sinking lower in her seat, she said, "I guess I've been caught red-handed." She shrugged helplessly. "I don't know why I told you those things. They just kind of slipped out. It didn't seem so bad at the time. . . ." She faltered.

Suddenly Lisa laughed, grabbing Roni's wrists and shaking her arms up and down. "Relax," she cried. "I think it's a riot."

"You do?" Roni stared in disbelief.

"Are you kidding? You really had us going, you know. I mean, everyone believed you."

"You did?" Roni glanced at her quizzically. "And you're not mad?"

Lisa scoffed. "I couldn't care less."

"You mean it? You're really not angry?"

Lisa made a ridiculous face at her. "It's too funny to get angry. You really pulled a good one—on us *and* on your roommates," Lisa said. "And I can see why you'd want to make fun of that Stacy. Is she a cool one or what?"

"Not always," Roni admitted uncomfortably. "I guess she was upset, huh? How did Evelyn meet her, anyway?"

"Someone knew she was your roommate, and Evelyn started asking her questions about you and your family. It didn't take much for us to figure it all out—that the things you told us really happened to your roommates. Stacy didn't think it was so funny, but I don't see what she's so steamed up about. It didn't hurt anyone." Calmly, Lisa took a sip of Roni's ginger ale. "I sure wouldn't want to room with her."

"Terry will be furious when she hears I told you about her brother's death that way. She never tells anyone."

Lisa looked at Roni strangely. "What's the big

deal? It doesn't make any difference to me. I don't care about her dead brother or Stacy's lush of a father."

Roni squirmed. Somehow Lisa wasn't making her feel any better. "Zack doesn't know about this, does he? Did you tell him I made those things up?"

Lisa shrugged. "I haven't seen much of Zack since we got back."

"I know." She hesitated. So far, Zack hadn't called her, but she didn't want Lisa to know that. "I called him a couple times, just to say hello, but he was out."

"It happens," Lisa said philosophically. "You'll run into him sometime."

Roni frowned. She'd expected to do more than run into him sometime—she thought he'd at least have called by now. And if Lisa had seen him, she could have mentioned Roni to him and found out why he hadn't called her. Still, Roni was just as glad they didn't talk. That meant that for now, at least, he didn't know about the stories she'd told.

Lisa looked bored. "Zack would think it was funny, too."

"Stacy didn't," Roni reminded her.

"Who cares about her? She has no sense of humor."

Roni dropped her head into her hands. "I can't believe I did that. How do I get into these things?"

"Oh, lighten up." Lisa opened one of Roni's notebooks, laughing at the doodles scribbled in the margin. "Great notes," she joked. "I hope you studied for your exams from something besides these."

Roni snatched the notebook away, slamming it shut. "Aren't you ever serious?"

"Why should I be?" Lisa challenged. "What difference would it make if I was?"

"I don't know," Roni said, backing down. *What good would it do*? Still, Roni felt uncomfortable. "Maybe I'm just touchy because I haven't seen Zack yet," she said finally.

"Probably," Lisa agreed. "Look, do you want to come back to my room and then we'll hit the library? I've got to get some work done."

Roni laughed. The amount of work Lisa did in the library was pitiful. Lisa's favorite spot was a table on the second floor, far away from the other tables and study carrels. It had a view of both the elevator and the second-floor stairwell, and no one could get in or out without her seeing them. Nobody ever complained about the noise she made while gabbing with people, so her study nights almost always turned into parties. Afterward, Roni never regretted wasting the evening there. Eagerly, she gathered her things together and followed Lisa back to her room. They had a glass of sherry, then hit the library. It was almost empty.

"I guess everyone's taking a break," Roni mused. "Relaxing after midterms."

"Weren't they awful?" Lisa asked as she pulled out a chair and collapsed into it. "I hope you did better than me."

"I'm not worried," Roni assured her. "I pulled two all-nighters and crammed really hard. I'll do okay." Checking her list of assignments, she realized she needed a book from the third floor. "I've got to go upstairs a minute," she said. "Save me a seat if things get lively here, okay?"

Lisa promised she would and Roni took the stairs to the third floor two at a time. The real grinds studied here—the stacks were so quiet you could hear a pin drop! Roni squeezed down the narrow aisle between the shelves of books, careful not to disturb the students who were working in the carrels that lined either side of the room. She found the stack she needed and pulled several books from the shelf. As she studied them, someone tapped her on the shoulder. "Hi, stranger," she heard.

"Zack!" She was so glad to see him she nearly yelled.

"Shh!" He put a finger to his lips, laughing. "Hi, Roni. How've you been?"

"Fantastic," she said flippantly. He was wearing a beat-up old sweatshirt that was so faded it was almost white. But on him it looked terrific. She couldn't help staring. It felt really good to see him again.

"I can't believe I haven't bumped into you until now," she said, carefully hiding any trace of eagerness in her voice. "I've seen Lisa every day."

"I've been pretty busy. Mostly here in the library," Zack told her.

"We've been here, too!" Roni exclaimed. "Lisa and I always sit in front of the elevators on the second floor."

Zack nodded. "That explains it. I never go down there."

Roni nodded also, playing it casual. He wasn't acting as though he'd missed her very much. "So, get my messages?" she asked, keeping her tone casual.

Zack lowered his eyes. "Uh ... yeah. Lately things have been pretty hectic—you know, exams came up so quick."

Roni felt as if she'd been slapped. He'd admitted it: He hadn't even tried to get in touch with her. "I see," she said stiffly. "Well, vacation was fun, anyway. I had some good laughs. Maybe I'll see you around again someday." She felt like screaming and crying at the same time. Blood pumped into her cheeks and she turned quickly so he wouldn't see.

Zack grabbed her by the arm, holding her in place. "Roni, wait." He turned her to face him, but looked down, unable to look her in the eye.

"Why?" she demanded shakily. "There's nothing between us. I knew that all along."

Zack seemed to struggle with himself. He loosened his grip on her arm, but didn't let go completely. It was as if he was afraid she might bolt. "We have to talk. Please?"

Roni wanted to run away. She was furious and embarrassed. "About what?" she asked, warily.

Zack's face looked tortured. "Just come back to my carrel for a minute, okay?"

She shrugged and let him lead her to a table in the far corner. She couldn't believe the stack of books, notebooks, and file cards on the desk.

"Looks like you're a real student." She examined a book. "Contemporary literary criticism, my favorite topic," she joked sarcastically. "That reminds me, do you happen to know a girl named Maddie

Lerner from your creative writing class? She says you're pretty good."

Zack actually grinned, looking pleased. "I'm not going to contradict a lady. How do you know Maddie, anyway?"

"My roommate Sam knows her."

"Maddie's very smart. And talented."

"Sounds like you're made for each other," Roni said, suddenly cold. "Except for on vacations. You're not the serious student, then, are you, Zack? Then you're Mr. Party Animal, out for laughs. What would Maddie think?" Her joke fell flat. She didn't have the heart to laugh, and Zack just stared at her.

"I have a confession to make," he said at last, taking a deep breath. "Roni, I hope you don't take this the wrong way, but . . . I purposely didn't call you once we got back to school."

Roni felt her cheeks flame. "No one said you had to." She tried to run away, but Zack caught her and held her firmly.

"Wait, don't do this. Please. We had fun in Daytona, but things are different here. School is important to me, and I need to work hard."

"And you think I would stop you." She wrenched out of his grip. "Well, guess what, Zack Cooper—school is important to me, too."

"Is it?" he asked. "Or is it just another excuse for a party?"

She turned her head, refusing to answer.

"Roni, please try to understand. Things were different in Daytona. I play so hard on vacations because I work so hard the rest of the time. Sure, I was wild down there, but I'm different here. I didn't think you'd like this side of me."

Roni tossed her head defiantly. "Oh, you mean I'm just some bimbo who'd get in your way at school? Thanks, but I don't need your insults."

"Look," he said, looking straight into her eyes. "I'm not part of Lisa's crowd. I can't party all the time and study, too. I thought you'd expect me to be able to do both."

"Who says I expect anything from you? Oooh, you make me so angry!" she cried.

"Roni, please. If you only knew how much I think about you. I tried not to, but . . ."

Roni knew she should leave. She'd never been so insulted in her life. He deserved to be slapped, or worse. To her amazement, however, she heard herself saying, "You thought about me?"

"Constantly."

Her heart leaped. But then she remembered his cruel words. "Well, for your information, Mr. Cooper, I'm not a bad student myself. Some people can study *and* have fun."

"Maybe you're right." Zack hesitated, then reached for her hand. Roni let him take it. It was unbelievably comforting just to hold hands with him.

Zack's voice was almost a whisper. "I just want things straight between us. I want us to see a lot of each other."

Roni couldn't believe her ears. "See a lot of each other?"

He slipped his arms loosely around her. "I kept telling myself we were wrong for each other, but

. . . there's something about you. . . ." He pulled her tightly to him and kissed her.

Her eyes shut, Roni felt some tension inside her let go. She hadn't admitted how tense she was, worrying and wondering if she'd ever see Zack again. The kiss ended and they stared at each other in a daze. Finally, Roni broke away.

"You have work to do," she said, her voice wavering.

Zack frowned in confusion. "What's wrong?"

"I'm not sure if I want a . . . a friend who studies all the time. I want to be with someone who has time for me."

Zack looked shocked. "That's a switch. I never worried about me being right for you." He shoved his hands in his pockets and looked at the floor.

Roni smiled, but pretended to be shocked. "You mean you have faults, too? I'm stunned."

Zack looked back up and grinned. He reached up and switched off the carrel light. "You're right, you know. Maybe I could rearrange my schedule. For now, would you like to take a walk?"

Roni smiled happily. "Sure." Roni hesitated. "Zack, as long as we're confessing faults, there's something else you should know about me." Now was the time to tell him about the stories she'd told in Daytona. It was better to get that understood right away.

"Stop—don't tell me a thing." Zack brushed his lips against hers. "I want to find out everything about you . . . my own way." He hugged her hard, making her laugh.

"Be serious, it's about spring break. . . ."

"Forget spring break. Everything between us starts right here, now, from this moment on."

Zack held her close. Roni gazed into his eyes and there didn't seem to be any point in telling him things he didn't want to know. As he'd just said, their history together was just about to start.

"Now, about that walk . . ." Zack looped his arm over Roni's shoulder and pulled her close, kissing the tip of her nose. They didn't stop to chat with Lisa as they passed the second-floor landing.

Chapter 9

Roni stood just outside the entrance to the mail-room, nodding hello to everyone she knew. She had on her brightest knit top so that Zack would spot her before he saw anyone else. Finally, she saw him coming.

"Right on time," he said, tousling her coppery red hair. "You look great today."

"I feel great." She beamed at him, and Zack took her hand. Glancing quickly around, he lifted it to his lips for a kiss.

"I thought about you all last night," he told her. "Did you think about me?" She nodded and Zack lifted a strand of her thick auburn hair and twisted it around his finger. "Promise you'll think about me every night."

Roni laughed.

"I mean it," Zack said, smiling. "Tell me."

"That's silly. I'll probably *see* you every night."

"Promise me, anyway."

"Okay." She laughed. "I promise."

Zack leaned close and they kissed. "I also got a ton of work done last night," he joked, shaking his head. "Did you study after I left?"

"Not really," Roni admitted. "I hung out with Lisa for a while. I had to tell someone about us."

Zack held her hands in his, his expression serious. "You'll have to study sometime. I don't want going out with me to ruin your grades."

Roni laughed. "Don't worry about it. I'll have plenty of time to see you and work, too." She went to kiss him again, but he pulled back, frowning. "Zack, believe me, I partied all the time in high school and I still got good grades. You don't know me—I'm an ace crammer."

"Okay, I believe you," he said, holding up his hands in defeat. "Look, my seminar starts early today, so I've got to run. But I'll see you later, right? After dinner?"

"In the library," Roni confirmed.

"Okay." He kissed her lightly on the cheek, then jogged quickly across the commons, stopping once to turn and wave to her.

Roni hugged her books. Everything was so wonderful! The balmy spring weather, the lovely old brick college buildings, even the ordinary old mailroom! Calling a bright hello to three girls from her art history class, she made her way across the room to her mailbox. Spinning the combination lock, she fished out the letters from inside.

A letter from her mother. She knew what that would say: nothing. It would tell all about who was at the club and ask if Roni had enough clothes and if she needed anything. And a check, naturally. Besides that and some junk mail asking her to apply for some credit cards she already had, there were three white postcards.

Uh-oh. Roni felt a chill. She recognized those postcards: exam grades. She still couldn't get used to getting her grades in the mail. It made her queasy. But then, she had nothing to worry about.

The first card was from her freshman composition professor. Roni smiled because Zack had told her last night it was his favorite class. It wasn't hers, that was for sure. Even so, she had no worries there. She always wrote great essays. Flipping the card over, she stared at it in shock. There was a big blue D across it. She'd never gotten a D in English in her life. It was one of her best subjects.

She flipped over the next card: introductory sociology—another D! Roni felt her cheeks flame. She hid the card against her sweater. She hadn't expected anything like this! In high school, the worst she'd ever gotten were straight C's, and once in a while a C-minus from some teacher who didn't really know her.

She'd done well enough last quarter, too. What was wrong! Well, she told herself, sociology and freshman comp were required subjects. She hadn't wanted to take them, so they didn't really count. She wouldn't even pay attention. The last card was from her art history class. She knew she'd done well on that—art history was going to be her major. Holding her breath, she turned the card over. Another D!

Roni was stunned. She slammed her mailbox shut and slowly walked across the quad toward her dorm. Sociology was meeting that period, but she couldn't face it. How had this happened? Maybe it was all a mistake. She'd done the work, hadn't she?

She'd skimmed all the required reading, handed in a five-page paper, and crammed hard for the exam. What more did they want?

A terrible thought struck her. *Zack*! He'd think she was a bad student, a party girl who didn't study and was close to flunking out. He'd never want to go out with her now! Her heart sank. She couldn't possibly tell him about her grades. If he asked her, she'd just have to lie.

Or maybe that wasn't such a good idea. He might find out anyway. And besides, if she had to lie to keep him, it would never work out. Roni groaned. Not now! She wanted to scream. Everything was going so well! Five minutes ago she'd been walking on air, and now she felt disgraced.

She really wanted to get back to her suite—badly. Stacy or Sam would be there to talk to. Yes, a good long talk and a hot cup of coffee—maybe even some of Sam's mother's famous homemade cookies—that's what she needed.

Hurrying across campus, suite 2C never seemed more like home. When she pushed open the suite door, Sam and Stacy looked up from the couch. Pam, their resident counselor, was perched on the floor and they had been talking a mile a minute. All three fell silent as Roni entered the room.

"Oh, don't stop talking because of me," she said vaguely, heading for the coffee machine. *Good, enough for a cup*, she thought. She filled her mug, grabbed a cookie, and settled into the easy chair, staring into space. The others exchanged uneasy glances and Roni looked up.

"Well, go on. It sounded like you were discussing

something serious. Don't mind me."

Pam stood, brushing off her jeans. "I'll let you all work this out yourselves," she said, pulling the door to the suite closed behind her as she left.

Roni looked at her roommates curiously. "Work what out? Something's awfully mysterious in here—what?"

"Oh, did you notice something?" With a haughty expression, Stacy began smoothing her already smooth blonde hair.

Sam shot Stacy a warning look. "There's something we needed to ask Pam's advice about," she began carefully.

"Oh, what?"

"Don't act so innocent," Stacy barked at Roni. "You know what we're talking about. How could you do it?"

Astounded, Roni set down her mug. "Huh? Do what? I'm not on academic probation, am I?"

"Probation? What are *you* talking about," Sam asked.

"My grades." Reluctantly, she showed them the postcards. "Pretty awful, huh?"

Sam studied the cards silently. Stacy glanced at them and sniffed. "What did you expect? You never study."

"Give me a break!" Roni cried. "I study as much as you do. I really thought I'd do well this term."

"How could you believe that?" Stacy asked coldly.

"I did believe it."

"Stop it, you two," Sam said, leaning toward Roni's chair from her seat on the couch. "Look, I'm sorry you're upset about your grades, but Stacy has a point. You can't expect good grades if you don't work for them."

"But I did! I worked as hard as ever. I stayed up all night for those exams. I worked as hard as I ever did in high school."

"There's a big difference between high school and college," Sam reminded her patiently.

"Right." Stacy nodded. "You can't just skate by on reputation here. These professors don't care who your parents are."

Roni stiffened angrily. "You're one to talk! You never worked hard in your life. And no one ever did me special favors because of my parents. I got good grades in high school because I earned them."

Sam laid a hand on Roni's arm. "I believe you, Roni. But I've seen the way you study. Half the time you're listening to records or watching TV. That just won't cut it here. I hate to see you mess up, too. You're smarter than that."

"I'm glad someone thinks so."

Stacy threw her a disgusted look. "What did you expect, Roni? A pat on the back? Or maybe a big present from your father—*the senator*."

Roni stared at her, then clapped a hand to her forehead. "Now I get it. I forgot that you bumped into Lisa. This is about the stories I told her, isn't it?" She smiled soothingly at Stacy. "They didn't mean anything, believe me. And Lisa couldn't care less."

"Don't bother to apologize," Stacy said in a hard voice. "I enjoy being made fun of."

"I didn't make fun of you," Roni insisted. "I didn't

mean to do anything to you. It meant nothing, honest."

"It's not nothing to me," Stacy said, her tone cold.

"Okay, I'm sorry."

Stacy remained stone-faced. "How could you? I don't really care for my sake, but what about poor Terry? She'd really be upset if she heard you'd told a stranger about her father being an alcoholic, and all that stuff about her brother's accident, pretending it all had happened to you. You had no right."

"We won't tell Terry. She's not even here anymore! If you don't tell her, she'll never know."

"I see," Stacy fumed. "Terry isn't here, so no harm done? I happen to consider Terry my friend. I guess you don't, though." She looked at Sam. "This is just what I was telling Pam about."

"Pam?" Roni faced Sam. "What's Pam got to do with this?"

Sam exchanged glances with Stacy. "We asked Pam to talk to us. Things have been really different since Terry left, and we needed a sounding board."

"I know. I miss her, too," Roni said. "It feels a little empty here without her. In fact, it's kind of crazy. I mean, we're so different, I never thought I'd like a grind like her." She frowned, thinking of Zack. Lately, she'd gotten involved with a lot of real grinds.

Stacy put her hands on her hips. "Can't you stop thinking about yourself for one minute? We were talking about Terry's feelings, not yours."

"She was my roommate. I'm the one who misses her the most," Roni said.

"You don't act like you even know she's gone."

"Why? Because I spend time with Lisa instead of always being here with you? Well, she happens to be a friend, too."

Stacy gaped at Roni. "Lisa didn't even know who you really were! She didn't know one true thing about you. What kind of friendship could you possibly have?"

Roni rolled her eyes. "Would you forget those stories I told her? That was just for fun. Anyway, Lisa knows what I'm like by how I act now."

Stacy scoffed. "Right, I forgot the campus lush was so sensitive," she muttered.

Roni sprang to her feet. "Don't call her that!"

"Roni," Sam said gently, "that's another thing we're worried about. We think Lisa may have a real drinking problem. Terry agrees, and she knows the signs to look for with alcoholism."

Roni stared at her roommates as if they'd gone crazy. "Lisa likes to have a good time, and she has more fun a little high than when she's completely sober, that's all."

"A little high!" Stacy laughed bitterly.

Sam frowned in concern. "What about you, Roni? Do you feel the same way?"

"I'm not stupid, Sam. I know drinking is no game. But Lisa is in control, too. She can stop anytime she wants."

"Sounds a little like Terry's dad," Stacy said. "Terry says he always used that line. The trouble was, he never even tried to stop."

"Lisa is not Terry's father, and you guys are being ridiculous." Roni clenched her fists. "I think you're both just jealous. You wish Lisa was your friend, and you're jealous that she's a junior and she likes me."

"No, thanks," Stacy said. "I don't need friends like Lisa. And I don't like you when you act like her. You embarrassed Terry to tears in that restaurant in Daytona. It was her last night with all of us and you ruined it. You acted like a sloppy drunk, and that's the worst thing anyone could do to Terry. You, of all people should know that."

Roni was stung. "A sloppy drunk! Look, Stacy, I don't know what your problem is, but don't take it out on me. I didn't do anything to you."

"You told lies about me."

Sam interrupted, pleading with both of them to calm down. "Okay," she said when they were all sitting again, "let's just forget about that night at the restaurant. We're not trying to hurt or embarrass you."

"Why should we care about her feelings?" Stacy exclaimed. "She doesn't care about ours."

"That's not true!" Roni cried. "I care a lot."

Sam took a deep breath. "You have to admit, Roni, over the whole vacation you either ignored us or acted bored when were around. That really hurt."

"But that was vacation. I did what I wanted and you guys did what you wanted. It's different now."

"What if we wanted to spend more time with you?" Sam asked.

"Oh," Roni said contritely. "I didn't think—"

"You never think," Stacy muttered. "Like the way you suddenly decided to drive back with Lisa."

"It made more sense that way," Roni protested.

"You didn't have to bug me about being up on time. I probably did you a favor."

"Not really," Sam said reasonably. "Actually, we were just worried. Suppose we'd left without you and then Lisa forgot about offering you a ride back? What if you were stuck down there?"

"She wouldn't forget," Roni insisted. But she felt uneasy—Lisa had forgotten half the things she'd done at the drive-in and the sunrise breakfast.

Sam went on talking. "We didn't know what to do, Roni. We were afraid to leave without you, so finally, we checked at Lisa's bungalow. Your stuff wasn't there so we just assumed you'd already left and everything was fine."

"And see, it was fine!" Roni cried. "Is this a guilt trip? What's the big deal?"

"Forget it, Sam." Stacy stood up. "She doesn't know how to be considerate of other people."

Angry tears came to Roni's eyes. "Is that so? Well, there's no law that says roommates have to be friends anyway."

"Great!" Stacy cried as she marched to her room. "Because it's a lost cause." She slammed the door.

"You should apologize to her," Sam told Roni softly.

"Me, apologize?" Roni nearly shouted, choking back tears. "How could you and Stacy talk about me to Pam behind my back? It's so humiliating."

Roni bit her lip to keep from crying. She needed desperately to talk about her problems with someone, but all she got was criticism!

Sam took a deep breath. "All I'm saying is, with

Terry gone, I really miss you. We used to do everything together."

Roni stood stiffly. "There's such a thing as too much togetherness," she said. "All you guys have done is dump on me. It's as if everything is my fault! It's not! It's not my fault."

Grabbing her purse and sweater, she headed for the door. "Stacy's right—roommates don't have to be friends. If you think about it, what do we have in common anyway?"

The tears really came as she ran down the stairs. She could hear Sam calling after her, but she kept right on going. She needed a real friend, someone who would really understand.

Chapter 10

Roni felt lower than ever. Now even Sam and Stacy were against her! If only she could talk to Zack. He would listen, and he'd understand. Maybe she could pull him out of his seminar. Then she remembered—her grades. Forget it. Zack would be disgusted with her if she told him she'd gotten three D's. What a mess! When she spotted Lisa coming out of the commons, Roni felt so relieved she almost started crying again.

"Lisa!" she called, crossing the quad. "I'm so glad to see you! Boy, have I got big problems."

Lisa linked arms with her. "Come on up to my room. I'll give you something to help your problems."

Roni sighed deeply. "A drink would be good right now."

When they got there, Lisa's room was a mess. Automatically, Roni started straightening up—something she rarely did in her own room. But there was something about Lisa that made Roni want to take care of her.

Lisa got out two glasses and poured some of her special sherry into them. Roni sipped hers slowly. It was a little too sharp, but she would never criticize Lisa's favorite drink.

"I'll bet your problems look smaller already," Lisa said, grinning at Roni over the rim of her glass.

Roni shook her head. "I need to talk, Lis. I don't even know where to start." The tears came back and Roni covered her face with her hands, crying harder than she had in years. "It's . . . oh, everything," she choked out between sobs. "Sam and Stacy are on my case . . . we just had a gigantic fight. Then there's my grades . . . and Zack. . . ." She broke down again.

"Hey, take it easy. Here, have some more." Lisa filled Roni's glass to the rim. Dutifully, Roni took another sip and set the glass down, wiping her eyes dry.

"My grades are bad—I mean *really* bad. If I tell Zack, what'll he think? What if he hates me?"

"He won't hate you," Lisa assured her.

"But he wasn't going to call me after vacation. He said he thought I wasn't serious girlfriend material."

Lisa waved her glass in the air. "So who needs him? Forget him if he doesn't want you. You're great the way you are."

"I can't forget him, Lis," Roni admitted. "And I don't want to. What am I going to do?"

Lisa finished her drink. "Damn!" she said. "It's empty." She held the bottle in front of Roni's face. "Look—gone."

"I don't want any more," Roni said. "Come on, help me figure out what to do about Zack."

"I know!" Lisa's face brightened. "We can go out for more!" She grabbed her jeans jacket and pushed her arms into the sleeves. "It's not that far. Come on, let's go."

"I really can't leave campus," Roni said. "I'm supposed to meet Zack later. Forget about that stuff, will you? I need advice."

"I know, but we'll come right back and then we can talk some more. We'll get it all straightened out, I promise," Lisa assured her.

Roni hesitated. "What time is it?"

"What difference does that make? It'll take us ten minutes." Lisa paused for a moment, thinking. "Except, that we can't walk to the liquor store, and Ray took his car into Atlanta tonight. Who else has a car?"

Reluctantly, Roni told her that Stacy always let them use her car. "She keeps a spare set of keys in the suite, but I can't really ask for them now. We just had a big fight."

"Then don't ask. She'll never even know."

"I can't do that! She's mad enough at me already."

"Forget her, she's a pain. I didn't like her at all."

Roni rolled her glass back and forth with her fingers. She was mad at Stacy right now, and Sam, too, but they weren't as bad as Lisa made them seem.

"Do this one little favor, please," Lisa asked sweetly. "Just take me to the store and then we'll come right back. No big deal."

Roni shook her head. "It's not a good idea."

Lisa frowned. Then a smile spread across her face. "If we go out, you could get a present for Zack. You know, something silly. He'd like that, wouldn't he?"

Roni wavered. She would love to get Zack a present—it might help. Maybe then he wouldn't take this grades business so seriously.

Lisa added sympathetically, "You're not feeling too sure of Zack right now, are you?" Roni shook her head. "Poor kid. You deserve a break."

"Okay," Roni said. "I'll ask Stacy for the keys. But just be ready for her to say no."

They hurried to the freshman dorm compound. Leaving Lisa waiting in the stairwell, Roni gingerly pushed open the door to her suite. She poked her head inside. It was very quiet. Stacy and Sam might still be at dinner, or maybe they were reading in their rooms. Roni hesitated. She didn't like feeling so sneaky, but she needed the keys right away. . . .

She told herself Stacy probably wasn't even mad anymore, not very mad, anyway. The spare keys were usually in a drawer in the coffee table. On tiptoes, Roni entered the living room, holding her breath as she slid open the drawer. The keys were there! She grasped them tightly to keep them from clinking together, then closed the drawer. Slipping back into the hallway, she nearly ran to the stairwell.

"Got them!" She let out a long breath, feeling like a criminal.

"Let's get out of here," Lisa said wildly. She giggled.

"Shh!" Roni said. Her heart was beating fast as they ran down the stairs, and Roni started giggling, too. It was so silly, stealing something she was allowed to have. Still, she was really relieved that no one had seen her.

They ran all the way to the parking lot. Stacy's Mercedes was parked in the front row. Roni unlocked the doors and she and Lisa scrambled in.

"Nice car!" Lisa exclaimed, running her fingers over the plush upholstery. "She lets you borrow this?"

"Yeah," Roni said. "Stacy can be generous sometimes."

Driving extra carefully because she felt guilty about the way she'd taken the car, Roni headed downtown. When she pulled up in front of the liquor store, Lisa gasped.

"They're closed!"

"I guess it's later than we thought," Roni said. "Oh, well. We can still get Zack a little present. Let's go back to the mall."

"No!" Lisa put a hand on her arm. "We can try someplace else."

"There aren't any other liquor stores. Besides," she added, "I want to get the car back before Stacy finds out it's gone."

"A few more minutes won't matter," Lisa began with a scowl. "Wait, I've got an even better idea. We can go to the Mackinak Roadhouse."

"The what?" Roni asked skeptically.

"It's fantastic! You'd love it. They have live music and dancing every night."

"I thought we were just getting a bottle. And I wanted a present for Zack."

"This is a present for Zack," Lisa said quickly. "We'll call him up and tell him to meet you there. It'd be very romantic—surprising him this way."

Roni hesitated. "But I wanted to get the car back. . . ."

"You can tell Zack about your grades while you're dancing. Give him a drink or two and dance slow. After that it won't seem so bad."

"Maybe you're right. It might work."

"Sure it will," Lisa told her. "Besides, I just got a craving for an ice-cold Margarita, and I can't mix that in my room. So see, it works out for everyone."

After she thought about it, the plan appealed to Roni. She and Zack could dance a little, and then have a quiet talk. From the way Lisa had described the Roadhouse, it sounded really romantic. Things wouldn't seem so bad in that kind of atmosphere. "You know," she remarked, "I'm beginning to wonder what I was so upset about. I took those exams before I knew Zack liked me. No wonder I was distracted—I was worrying if he'd ever call me again."

"And he'll love that story," Lisa assured her. "All you have to do is play up how upset you were, and promise to work harder from now on. He won't be able to resist."

"Lisa, this is a brilliant idea," Roni said happily. "Which way to the Roadhouse?"

They followed country roads for several miles until Lisa finally pointed out the huge, old brick house. Originally, it was an inn for travelers, and it still had the authentic Colonial look that Roni loved. There were also big old trees dripping Spanish moss lining both sides of the road out front.

"It's so quaint!" she cried. "I love it! So will Zack."

Lisa shivered. "It's gotten chilly suddenly. Let's go inside and warm up."

Lisa hurried inside but Roni held back, absorbing the details of the architecture. By the time she entered the narrow hallway that led to the main room, Lisa was already sitting down at a table. Roni hurried over, pulling out her chair as the waiter came over to tell them about cover charges and minimums.

"No problem," Lisa told him. "Bring us each two drinks at once and then we won't have to worry about the minimum anymore."

Roni laughed. "Two at once?"

"Why not? We're going to have them anyway, aren't we?"

"I guess so."

Lisa ordered two Margaritas and Roni decided to have the same. She also asked the waiter for a menu. "I'd love a sandwich or something," she said. "Aren't you starved?"

"You go ahead and eat. I'm not hungry."

"Come on, you have to eat something. You haven't even had dinner. All that drinking on an empty stomach . . ." Roni stopped talking as Lisa shot her a dirty look.

"What are you, my mother? I'm not hungry, okay?"

"Sorry. Geez, you don't have to snap." Roni sat back in her chair. "I've been yelled at enough today."

"Just don't tell me what to do," Lisa said crossly.

"I said I was sorry." Annoyed, Roni picked up her

purse. "I'd better call Zack and let him know where to find me."

Lisa nodded, looking for the waiter and her drinks.

Roni left a message for Zack with some guy in his dorm. Too bad—he was probably studying already. Dialing again, she tried the library, explaining to the boy who answered where Zack usually sat.

"Sorry," the boy said in a crisp tone. "I can't get a student unless it's an absolute emergency."

"But I know he's there," Roni said. "He's on the third floor, the last carrel on the left."

"I'm busy at the desk," the boy told her. "I'm sorry, but I can't leave my post except for an emergency."

"This *is* an emergency!" Roni lied. "Uh . . . someone's really sick and he has to come right away."

"Is this a prank?"

"Of course not!" Roni pulled the receiver away from her ear and glared at it. "Look, just give Zack Cooper a message that he should come to the Mackinak Roadhouse on Route 108."

"Isn't that a bar?" he asked suspiciously.

"Yes, it is," Roni said impatiently. "We were eating here and his . . . uh . . . sister got sick. His sister Roni. Tell him he has to come and get her."

Sounding unconvinced, the boy finally gave in.

"Just tell him to get here as soon as possible. It's urgent." She repeated the address to the boy, then hung up. Hurrying back inside, she saw her sandwich had arrived. She attacked it hungrily. "I hope Zack gets the message," she told Lisa between bites. "I'd better try again in a little while."

"What'd you tell them?"

"I said his sister was really sick and he has to come help." She and Lisa both laughed.

"I hope Zack doesn't have a sister," Lisa joked. "He might really get worried."

"I said it was Roni, and I'm sure he doesn't have a sister named Roni. He has to know it's me."

Lisa shrugged. "Don't worry about it. The band is fantastic, huh?"

While she had been on the phone, the band had started it's first set. Pulsing music filled the room.

She would call Zack again later, but in the meantime, there was nothing wrong with enjoying the music, was there?

"This is my favorite kind of place," Roni told Lisa. "All this old wood and bricks and stuff. Did you see the blacksmith shop tools hanging in the hallway? I think it's cool how they hung up things like tools and machinery as decoration. Someday I'd like to have an old barn and convert it into a house—you know, with sleeping lofts, and huge windows."

Lisa nodded.

"I have lots of ideas like that to fix places up. It's the one thing I liked about my parents. They never cared how much they spent on decorators. Once I did the playroom over in a Mediterranean style. Yuk! It was so ugly. I hated it. But they were cool. They just ordered all new furniture." She laughed, remembering.

Lisa wasn't paying attention, though. "Where is that waiter? I could use a refill."

Roni glanced at the table in surprise. Lisa had

already finished both her drinks! "That was fast."

"So? Where is he?" Lisa grumbled.

Roni pushed one of her drinks across the table. "Here, have mine."

"Don't you want it?"

"I still have another one. Anyway, what's the rush? I don't know how long it will be until Zack gets here."

Lisa didn't say anything as she reached across the table and took Roni's drink.

"What a day!" Roni said, crunching the last of her potato chips. "Not only do I have my roommate's car, which she doesn't know I've taken, but now my new boyfriend is about to find out I'm everything he doesn't want me to be. Why does everything always go wrong at once?"

"Huh?"

"I guess things always look worse at night. It will seem better in the morning. Just let me get through tonight."

Lisa nodded her head in time to the music. "Did you say something?"

Roni let out a short laugh. "Not much. Let's just try to have a good time." She sipped her drink. Lisa turned to signal the waiter for a refill.

"Better order another one," Lisa said. "C'mon, drink up."

"I am drinking. You're beginning to sound like my mother when she used to bug me to finish my milk. Only milk is good for you."

"This is good for you, too," Lisa countered. "It'll make all your problems go away. You'll feel much better."

"Is that why you drink so much?" Roni asked curiously. "To make yourself feel better?"

"I don't drink *that* much," Lisa denied.

Roni grinned. "You drink more than anyone I know." She shrugged. "I wish it could make my problems go away, but it won't."

"Try harder," Lisa joked. "I do, and I have no problems. Not a care in the world."

Roni looked at her friend seriously. "Lisa," she said in a quiet tone, "if anything is ever bothering you, I'm here for you."

Lisa frowned at her. "Don't play games with my head, all right? Nothing's bothering me."

"I was just trying to be a friend," Roni said, surprised at Lisa's mean tone.

"A friend would shut up." Lisa pushed her glass toward Roni. "Here, have some more."

The waiter arrived with their refills. Roni had no sooner finished a Margarita than another appeared. It was just like back in Daytona—only this wasn't as much fun. She glanced anxiously at her watch. "Zack should have been here by now. It's almost time for the library to close."

Lisa shrugged, her expression sour. "Maybe he doesn't want to come. He's a goody-goody, anyway. Who needs him?" She beat on the table in response to the music, loudly and not in the right tempo.

"Lisa, keep it down. People are looking at us."

"Who? Those guys over there?" Lisa winked at the next table. One of the boys winked back at her. Lisa giggled and gave him a little wave. "He's cute," she confided to Roni.

Roni laughed indulgently. Her head felt awfully

light—she hadn't meant to drink so much. She pressed her hands against her temples and shook her head. *Maybe Zack shouldn't come*, she thought suddenly. *Maybe he shouldn't find me like this.*

Her stomach lurched in anxiety. "I almost wish I'd never met Zack," she whispered. "I hate worrying like this. I hate feeling like I did something wrong!"

"Keep drinking," Lisa urged.

"It's not fair," Roni declared. "I didn't do anything wrong on purpose." Suddenly she felt like crying again. "I was so happy in Daytona. Why couldn't it have stayed like that?"

"Nothing good lasts," Lisa said bitterly. "You're better off knowing that right from the beginning."

"But Zack really liked me. He really accepted me." Roni was getting a headache.

Lisa made an angry gesture. "Oh, who cares about Zack?" she cried loudly.

"I made a big mistake, coming here tonight." Roni rubbed her forehead. "I shouldn't have taken Stacy's car. Stacy was so mad at me. She'll tell Zack, and then he will know I'm too wild. He won't like me. He won't like me at all."

Roni pushed her drink away. She couldn't think straight anymore.

Lisa jumped up. "Let's dance."

Roni stared at her and then giggled. *Why not?* she thought. She loved to dance. She loved to have fun.

Lisa pointed at the guys at the next table. "They'll dance with us."

Sure, that's what's wrong with me, Roni told herself as the boys stood up. *I haven't been myself lately. I . . . I need to have fun. I . . . I need some excitement.*

In seconds she was on the dance floor with some guy. Roni loved dancing more than anything. She never wanted to sit down. It was a blast the way guys kept cutting in. She was the life of the party. This was more like it!

After what seemed like only minutes she took a break. "This place is fantastic," she told Lisa.

"I told you," Lisa bragged. She grabbed the waiter by the arm. "Two more Margaritas for this table."

"Sorry, ladies. We already had last call. We'll be closing soon."

"But I want another drink."

"I told you, you missed last call. It's closing time."

"You didn't run out of liquor, did you? Won't you just get me one more drink?" Lisa pleaded.

"I think you've had enough already," the waiter said politely.

Lisa scowled. "I had two drinks, three at most."

"If you say so," the waiter muttered. "Look, I'm sorry but we're closing. No more drinks tonight."

Roni got to her feet. "Closing? You can't close," she protested. Her voice sounded funny, kind of distant, in her ears. She licked her lips and tried very hard to speak clearly. "Zack isn't here yet." She grabbed the waiter's hand, clinging to it as she swayed on her feet. "Zack is coming to get me."

"Listen, girls, I don't know who Zack is. All I know is, you have to leave." The waiter looked at Roni with concern. "Do you have a safe ride home?"

Her head was spinning as Roni gathered up her

things. "I can drive okay," she murmured. "Really, I'm fine."

Very carefully she headed toward the exit, trying to walk in a straight line. Lisa stumbled after her. The waiter watched them go.

Outside, Roni grabbed Lisa's arm. "Fooled him!" She giggled. Now it all seemed so funny. "I shouldn't drive. I'm really plastered." She dissolved into giggles.

Chapter 11

Roni wrenched open the driver's-side door and crawled onto the front seat of the car. On the passenger's side, Lisa wrestled with the handle, breaking a fingernail. She stood in the driveway cursing.

"Get in," Roni said, giggling. She sprawled across the seat, unlocking Lisa's door.

With a haughty look, Lisa flung the door open and flounced inside. Roni stabbed the key at the keyhole on the steering wheel. For some reason it wouldn't fit. Over and over, she twisted and thrust the key. Lisa tapped impatiently on the dashboard.

"What's taking so long?" Lisa asked crossly. She leaned over to slam her door and then flopped against the seat. Groaning, she shut her eyes.

"Whatever you do, don't pass out," Roni warned her, "You look like you might pass out."

With effort, Lisa raised her head. "Don't be stupid. I'm not even drunk."

Roni snorted. "You're as ripped as I am!" She took a deep breath and tried to think straight. "Maybe we should take a little nap. I'm too sleepy to drive." Then she frowned. "But we can't. We have to get back . . . find Zack. Because . . . because he didn't come here."

Lisa murmured something incoherent.

"Got to find Zack," Roni chanted. "Got to find Zack." She started the motor. Her head felt as if it weighed about ten tons, and something was wrong with her stomach, too. "Have to get back," she whispered over and over.

The car wheels spun on the loose gravel as she backed up. She jerked the wheel to the right and, miraculously, the car straightened out and moved backward.

"So far so good," Roni muttered. Her heart was pounding. "I'm fine, I'm fine," she told herself. "I had a lot to drink, but if I just take it easy, I'll be okay."

Lisa moaned on the seat next to her. "Wha'? What'd you say?"

"Come on, baby," Roni crooned to the car, ignoring Lisa. "That's it, good car. Nice and easy." Cautiously, she pulled out of the parking lot and into the middle of the road, leaving herself plenty of space to maneuver.

Her hands were tense on the wheel, and her neck ached from the effort of sitting up straight. Roni prayed the police weren't around anywhere, although in a funny way, that would be a relief. They'd make her stop driving. She'd be safe.

"I wish Zack would come," she whimpered. If Zack came now, he could take care of them. He would get them home. But there was no sign of the Jeep.

She heard a strange sound. Next to her, Lisa was

snoring softly. Rudely, Roni shook her. "Lis!—Lis, wake up! C'mon Lis—help me out here." But Lisa was dead to the world.

Headlights swept through the car from behind, making Roni's pulse race—Zack? Maybe the police? She swerved to the right and the other car speeded up, honking as it passed. In confusion, she watched it disappear down the road. Was she going too slow? She pressed harder on the gas pedal and the car jumped forward, heading for the stately oaks that lined the road. Panicked, she took her foot off the gas pedal completely and the car stalled. Oh, no!

"Stay calm," she muttered, "stay calm." She looked at Lisa, slouched against the door, and climbed over to fasten her seat belt around her. She moved back behind the wheel and fastened her own seat belt. "There, nice and safe," she murmured. "Got to take it slow and safe." Counting to ten, she inhaled slowly. She started the car again, this time keeping her speed down to a crawl.

It seemed to take forever to get back to Hawthorne, driving so slow. But a least they were in one piece. When Roni finally spotted the entrance gate, she closed her eyes in relief.

"Safe! We're safe!" She prodded Lisa. Lisa turned her head away.

There was only one more problem: The guard at the gate would want to check their ID's. Usually, Roni and her friends would stop to chat, kidding around. She knew he liked that. But not tonight. Tonight she couldn't risk letting him get close enough to smell her breath. Hers had to be bad, and Lisa's reeked. He could put her on report for sure!

With one hand, she fished in her purse, pulling out her ID card. Swerving the car close to the guard's station, she waved the card in the air, smiling as if she were perfectly in control. She pointed at Lisa, sleeping beside her, as if to say she couldn't stop because she wanted to get her sleepy friend back to the dorm right away.

The guard nodded and smiled back, waving her in. Roni managed a casual wave as she pulled onto the winding road that led around the Hawthorne campus.

Roughly, she reached over and shook Lisa's shoulder. "Get up. We're back."

Groggily, Lisa sat up. Running her hand through her hair, she grimaced. "Ugh! My mouth tastes awful. What happened? Did I fall asleep?

"Uh-huh. Out cold."

Lisa checked her watch. "Hey, it's early. We don't have to go home yet, do we?"

Grimly, Roni stared ahead of her. "I'm never doing this again. Never!" Tears of tension sprang to her eyes. "And you were no help at all!"

"What'd you want me to do?" Lisa peered out the window at the quiet campus. "It's dead around here. What a drag."

Roni ignored her, concentrating on the curving road.

"C'mon, Roni, let's go downtown and find some people, have some fun."

"I can't. I've got to find Zack. He never showed up."

"Zack? Show up where?" Lisa rubbed her eyes.

Roni shook her head in exasperation. "Don't you ever remember anything?"

Slowly, she made the turn onto the access road that led to the dorms. Narrow and winding, it passed over a low stone bridge that ran above a shallow creek. As they approached, Roni suddenly remembered how only the night before she and Zack had taken a walk and stopped here, leaning against the stone wall to toss twigs into the creek. It was one of those balmy nights when it was impossible to be inside. The air had smelled like spring flowers.

Zack. It was possible that he'd never gotten her messages. He might not know where she was. Or, worse, maybe they'd found him at the library and he was furious about the false emergency. He'd know it wasn't real. She bit her lip. She should never have gone out with Lisa. The phony emergency was a stupid idea. This whole night was a stupid idea.

Lisa pouted at Roni. "I don't want to go back yet! Turn around!" She grabbed at the wheel.

"Don't!" Roni yelled at her. "Hey, cut it out!"

Giggling wildly, Lisa lunged toward Roni and pulled on the wheel, trying to turn the car around. "Turn around!" she cried.

"Stop! Don't . . ." Roni yelled. Lisa reached her foot over and stomped down hard on the gas pedal. The tires squealed and the car lurched wildly.

Someone was screaming. Dimly, Roni realized it was her own voice. She was screaming because the car was skidding over the bridge. She saw everything very clearly—sort of in slow motion. The stone wall of the bridge seemed to slide slowly toward them, although Roni knew that was impossible. The bridge wasn't moving, it was perfectly still. It was the car that was moving. Smoothly, noiselessly, the car slid toward the stone wall. It felt so natural, as if it was meant to be. She wondered how badly they were going to be hurt. It was the last thing she thought about as the stones loomed up and the car hit the wall.

Chapter 12

Roni felt as if she were floating in a clear, blue void. She had no weight, no body to pull her down. Everything was crystal-clear, bathed by a glorious white light. She wanted to stay there forever, just floating. . . .

Then someone started moaning. Slowly, the feeling started to flow back into her body. Her head ached and there was a dull throb in her stomach. She began to realize those were her own moans she'd been hearing. Her eyes fluttered open, and the beautiful blue void was gone.

Where was she? She lifted a hand and it bumped into something cold and hard. Plastic, maybe? It felt like a wheel . . . the steering wheel! That's right, she was in a car. It was dark out, and the car wasn't moving. What was she doing in a parked car in the dark?

Struggling to sit up, her head throbbed sharply. Lifting a hand to her forehead, she felt something wet and warm. Blood! Her eyes widened in shocked surprise and then she remembered. Stacy's car . . . they were driving back . . . there was an accident . . . *Lisa!*

Turning her head to the side, she saw Lisa lying completely still on the seat beside her. Lisa's eyes were closed and she looked as if she were asleep. In a daze, Roni looked around. There was no longer any front to the car—just a mass of crumpled metal pushed against the stones. Where the fender should have been, pieces of battered chrome stuck up at odd angles. The windshield was shattered, and pellets of safety glass were all over the dashboard, her lap, and the front seat. The pellets were also scattered over Lisa, who looked deathly pale.

Roni's heart pounded. "Lisa!" Her voice was a harsh croak. "Lisa!"

Nothing. "Lisa, wake up!" she cried as loud as she could. It made her head hurt. She dropped back against the seat and closed her eyes, trying to catch her breath.

Lisa moaned softly. "What happened?"

"You're all right!" Roni cried in relief.

Lisa moaned. "Am I hurt?" She pressed a hand against her forehead. "Ouch!"

Roni began to cry softly. "Thank God! I thought you were dead. I thought we were both dead."

Lisa stared at her blankly.

Now Roni was beginning to remember everything. As the full horror hit her, the words began spilling out wildly.

"The stones . . . right there . . . and the bridge . . ." A coughing fit forced her to stop talking. Exhausted, she shut her eyes again. "Lisa, hold my hand. If you don't, I'm afraid I'll . . . I'll die."

Woodenly, Lisa laid her hand over Roni's. "What a mess," she murmured. She looked over at Roni, and her hand flew to her face. "Oh, my God!" she whispered. "You're all bloody!"

"Is it bad?" Roni asked in a panicky voice, afraid to move.

Lisa just stared, a look of shock on her face.

"Lisa! Am I okay?"

The color drained from Lisa's cheeks. Shakily, she reached out and lifted the matted hair away from Roni's face. She let the hair drop and fell back against her seat, taking deep breaths.

Roni swallowed deeply. "I must be okay," she said numbly. "If I'm talking I must be okay."

Gingerly, Roni touched her neck. Her muscles ached all across her shoulders. The broad ribbon of her seat belt was cutting into her skin. Then she began to laugh, her body aching each time she did. "My seat belt . . ." she said vaguely. "When did I buckle my seat belt?"

Relief flooded over her. If she hadn't fastened her seat belt, she would be as crumpled as the chrome and metal of the car.

Lisa listened wide-eyed to Roni's jagged laughter. "You're hysterical," Lisa muttered. "Must be shock."

"No," Roni said weakly. "No, it is funny. Too drunk to drive, but we're wearing our seat belts." Her laughter sounded crazily in her ears and she began shaking all over. It all came back to her now: The tense drive, struggling to keep the car under control, her relief at reaching the campus, and then the short, terrifying fight with Lisa. Even the slow-motion slide into the bridge. She couldn't stop shaking as she thought of it.

"That's right," Lisa whispered. "We were drinking

and we crashed. Oh, no!" She suddenly clawed at her door. "I've got to get out of here!"

"Lisa, it's all right. We're all right," Roni said. It seemed funny to feel so calm and logical. Maybe Lisa was right—maybe she was in shock.

Lisa pushed and scratched frantically at the door. "I've got to get out of here!" she began shrieking.

"Don't, Lisa, don't." Roni tried to get to Lisa to calm her down, but she was pinned behind the wheel. She wet her lips and tried to speak calmly. "Lisa . . . I can't move."

Lisa wildly brushed the glass pellets from her lap. She reached under the seat for her purse. "Got to go . . ." she started crying.

"Lisa, calm down. We're all right now."

Lisa's eyes were wide with alarm. She shrieked at Roni.

"Don't you understand? We're not all right! Security will come, maybe the police! I'm already on probation, Roni. If they find me drunk . . . I've got to get out of here."

Roni tried again to move, but her door was smashed in, impossible to open. "Please, Lisa," she begged softly. "You have to get help. I can't move. Lisa, help me!"

Lisa threw herself against the door, clawing at the handle. Finally the door cracked open, with a tearing sound. She turned to look at Roni. "I can't," she whispered harshly. "I'm sorry, Roni. I'm really sorry." She slid across the seat, squeezing through the opened door.

Roni summoned all her strength, but she was so weak. "Lisa! Lisa, wait!" she pleaded.

But Lisa was gone. Roni shut her eyes. She was all alone now. Around her, the crickets were making a racket. She noticed the soft rustling noise of the water pushing over loose stones in the creek below her. After resting a moment, she tried again to get out from under the wheel. It was no use.

"Help! Somebody!" she called weakly. Her voice was pathetically small against the silence of the night. "Please, somebody help me, please."

Far in the distance, she thought she heard the faint wailing of a siren. Then there were lights, too. If only she could yell, get their attention. But she was so tired. Too tired. Her eyes closed again.

"There's a girl in there!" a muffled voice shouted, waking Roni up. "Can't tell if she's alive. . . ."

Someone was next to her on the front seat, brushing away glass and rubble. Slowly, Roni's vision focused. She saw a uniform.

"Take it easy now," the man said kindly. His hand was around her wrist, feeling her pulse. "That's it, nice and easy." He peered at her face, his eyes concerned. "Can you tell me your name? Do you remember your name?" Gently but firmly, he was pressing her arms and legs, checking for broken bones.

Roni licked her lips again. "Roni . . . Roni . . . Veronica Davies," she said formally.

The ambulance man smiled. "Okay, Roni. Take it easy. I think you're going to be just fine."

"Is she all right?" a male voice asked.

"Zack!" Roni cried, struggling to sit up.

"Hold on, you're not going anywhere," the man told her. "He your boyfriend?"

Zack appeared at the car door, looking both worried and relieved. "Roni!—Roni . . . you're alive!" His voice broke.

She smiled weakly. "Yeah, I'm okay."

Together, the ambulance attendants managed to move back the front seat, freeing Roni from behind the steering wheel. They unhooked her seat belt and gently slid her from the car, placing her on a gurney. Carefully, they rechecked her vital signs, taking her pulse and blood pressure and listening to her breathing.

Zack stood there anxiously, waiting. "How is she?"

"Not too bad. Her pulse and respiration are almost normal, and the blood pressure is good." The attendant shone a light in Roni's eyes and nodded in satisfaction. "Not too dilated. I think she's going to be okay."

"I . . . I feel a little shaky still," Roni said.

The attendant patted her arm. "Of course you are. That was some collision. You totaled your car, I'm afraid."

"Stacy's car!" Roni gasped.

Zack leaned over her. "Forget about the car. Let's get you taken care of first."

"We'll take her to the college infirmary," the attendant told Zack. "She's stable enough that I don't think we need to go all the way to the hospital. You can come, if you're careful not to disturb her."

"I'll be careful," Zack promised.

A security guard pulled Zack aside, but Roni

heard them anyway. "Do you know who owns the car?"

"One of her roommates," Zack told him. "Stacy Swanson. She's in her room now. I was just there, looking for Roni."

Security asked Zack a few more questions and seemed satisfied with his answers. "After the infirmary checks her over, we'll have to ask more questions—in case the roommate presses charges, that kind of thing."

In the ambulance, Zack stroked Roni's hand. She was sick with worry about Lisa, but Zack wouldn't let her talk. "Rest, keep quiet," he told her, over and over.

Gratefully, she closed her eyes and rested. In the infirmary they took her pulse and blood pressure all over again. They wheeled her into a little room and took X rays of her head, and the doctor poked and prodded her absolutely everywhere. Then a nurse came in and took some blood. They were going to run a test to determine the level of alcohol in her blood, the nurse told her. Embarrassed, Roni looked away.

Finally, they let Zack come in and wait with her for the results.

Roni struggled to sit up. "Zack, I have to tell you something. . . ."

"Sit back," Zack ordered. "You have to rest."

"It's important." Roni reached for his hand.

"Shh! Not now," Zack said sternly.

Moments later, the doctor pushed aside the white curtain around her bed. "Good news," he said. "It's only a minor concussion. I talked with security, and from what they and your boyfriend say, it seems as if you only lost consciousness for a short time."

"That's right." Zack nodded. "I got there the same time the ambulance did. Her eyes were closed, but she answered me right away when I spoke to her."

"The attendants told me. That's a good sign," the doctor said.

"Yes, I know I was alert," Roni began "I told . . ."

"She told us she was fine," Zack finished.

Roni smiled weakly. She was really about to say she told Lisa to stay calm, to wait in the car until help came, but she caught herself. Roni was the only one who knew Lisa was in the car. She bit her lip to keep from telling the doctor.

He smiled kindly at her. "Your X rays are clear," he continued. "Lucky thing you were wearing that seat belt. You probably bumped your head on the windshield, and there might be some whiplash problems later, but it could have been a lot worse. You could have been thrown through the windshield into the wall, or into the creek. Who knows what would have happened—"

"Do you have to scare her this way?" Zack protested.

The doctor put his hand on Zack's shoulder. "She's going to think of all these things herself," he explained. "It's better to get them out of the way. She's still a bit dazed, you'll see. It will take awhile until the full impact of what happened hits her."

"Oh, I see," Zack said.

Roni hesitated. "Am I going to be all right?"

"No brain damage there, if that's what you're

worried about. Your vital signs are steady. All in all,
it's a pretty mild concussion."

"That's a relief." Zack sighed. Roni squeezed his
hand, grateful to have him there. She managed a
weak smile.

The doctor frowned slightly at both of them.
"The more serious problem is your blood-alcohol
level."

Roni flushed. "I know," she mumbled. His words
made her feel terrible, but Roni knew it was her
own fault. She looked at him, ashamed.

"I won't go into the legal aspects—you'll have to
deal with that later. But I will tell you that you're
one very lucky young woman. As intoxicated as
you were, it's lucky you didn't kill anyone."

Roni turned pale. The doctor was right, and she
knew it.

"I hope you learned your lesson," he went on.
"Drinking and driving is a dangerous game. You're
lucky to be alive yourself."

Roni's eyes burned with tears, and she nodded
mutely.

The doctor's tone softened. "I'm going to send
you back to your dorm in a while, providing there's
someone there to take care of you."

"I'll watch her," Zack promised. "And her roommates will help. They're very reliable."

"They are," Roni whispered. But would they even
want to take care of her now?

The doctor scribbled some words on a pad. "You
may have some headaches, so I'm giving you
something that will help. If the pain persists or gets
worse, call me immediately." He spoke to Zack. "I

don't expect any, but watch her for signs of fever and delirium. With any luck, though, she'll just sleep it off and that will be the end of it."

"How long should she stay in bed?" Zack asked anxiously.

"Probably just a day or two. She'll let you know when she's able," the doctor assured him.

Roni squeezed Zack's hand, expecting a comforting smile, but Zack looked away.

"I'll tell the nurse to send Security in to take a statement," the doctor told her.

"Security?" Nervously, she glanced at Zack.

"You had a serious car accident on campus. They'll need a complete account of everything that happened."

Roni closed her eyes, dismayed. She had promised not to tell about Lisa being in the car with her, but could she pull it off? She opened her eyes and found Zack watching her curiously. Anxiously, she reached for his hand.

The doctor noticed. "I'll give you two a moment alone together first."

"Thank you." The doctor left the room, and she turned immediately to Zack. "I'm so scared."

Zack pulled his hand away. "You should be!" He declared angrily. "What did you think you were doing, pulling a crazy stunt like that?"

Roni gazed at him in surprise. "I . . ."

Zack ran his hands through his hair. "Damnit, Roni!" he shouted. "You could have gotten killed!"

"I didn't think . . ."

"You *never* think!" Zack exploded. "That's the

whole problem." He sank onto the edge of the bed, his head in his hands.

Roni had never seen Zack angry like this. It frightened and confused her. A minute ago he'd seemed so concerned. Gingerly, she touched his shoulder, afraid he might pull away.

"Zack, don't be this way. Please . . ."

He stared at her. "I don't know what to do, what to think," he said. "Vacation was one thing. We were all a little crazy then. But I'd hoped you'd be different back on campus. You said you would be, and I believed you."

"I meant it."

"You meant it one minute, but the next you're off partying again, as wild as ever. Wilder, even." He grabbed her shoulders. "Drinking and driving is crazy! Do you think you're immortal or some- thing—that you can pull any stupid stunt and not pay the price? You totaled Stacy's car, and you could have been killed."

Roni didn't know what to say.

"I thought we were a couple now," Zack said quietly. "I thought that I mattered to you."

"You do!" Roni cried.

"No I don't. If you cared about me, you wouldn't take risks like this. You wouldn't be so careless. You have a responsibility to me now to take care of yourself. Same as I have a responsibility to you."

Roni began to weep quietly. "It . . . it was stupid to drive back. I know that."

"But you did it anyway."

"To . . . to see you," Roni said, sobbing.

Zack shook his head. "Is that how you think I like to see you?"

"No."

"You're right about that." Zack stared stonily at her. "You don't need to be drunk for me to like you. I like you more when you're sober."

"Oh, Zack," Roni pleaded, trying to find a way to make him understand. "Don't be angry."

"I'm so angry I'm going crazy!" He jumped up, rubbing a hand over his forehead. "It was dumb, Roni. Dumb."

"I see that now."

"Well, you should have seen it then." He crossed his arms and they looked at each other in strained silence. "Just let me explain—" Roni began.

At that moment, the man from Security came in to take Roni's statement.

Roni dried her eyes and tried to sit up.

The officer was abrupt and efficient, briskly taking down Roni's statement about the accident.

"Did you drive to the Roadhouse alone?" he asked her.

"Yes," she insisted. "I . . . I just needed to get away."

He frowned and Zack spoke up. "Actually, she left a message at my dorm, asking me to meet her there, but the place was closed by the time I got the message."

"Didn't the guy at the library give you my message?" Roni asked.

Zack shook his head. "Nobody told me. I went by her dorm," he continued to the man, "but she wasn't there yet. I woke up her roommates and they knew she was out, but not where she went. I took a walk to the Security gate to ask if she'd driven past. . . ." He paused, remembering. "Anyway, then the call came in about the crash. The guard called an ambulance. I . . . I had this weird feeling it was Roni—I don't know why, I just did. It was like a nightmare come true." Zack put a hand to his eyes. "Thank goodness she was all right," he murmured.

Roni felt a surge of hopefulness. Zack *did* care about her!

The man wrote everything down. "What exactly did you do after you left the Roadhouse?"

Roni swallowed. "I . . . uh . . . I was trying to drive slowly because I knew I'd been drinking. Just before the bridge, I lost control of the car and . . ." She shut her eyes, unable to think about it yet.

"That's enough for now." The man nodded. "We have the registration number of the car and all the pertinent information about you. There'll be a disciplinary hearing when the doctor says you're up to it."

Roni moaned. "A hearing?"

"Will the police be involved?" Zack asked.

"Since the accident occurred on campus, we can keep it within our jurisdiction, unless the owner of the car wants to press criminal charges against her, that is."

"Criminal charges?" Roni felt shocked.

"Possible auto theft, destruction of property."

"No!" Roni gasped. "Stacy lets us use her car."

"In that case, I guess you have nothing to worry

about. If it stays a college matter, we'll just take care of it here."

Roni nodded weakly. "I understand."

"Your most serious offense is driving while intoxicated," the security officer said. "That's the one to worry about." Flicking his pad shut, he left the room.

Roni stared blankly at the door after he left. *A disciplinary hearing!* She could be thrown out of school. And if Stacy or Stacy's parents pressed charges against her, she'd have a criminal record for the rest of her life.

Zack grabbed her hands. "As far as you know, is Stacy the type to press charges?"

"No, of course not. I don't think . . ." She started crying again. "Oh, I don't know!"

Zack looked grim. "Don't worry. I'll go to the student advisory council tomorrow and see what I can find out. Maybe they can help you."

"You don't have to do that for me, you know," Roni said gratefully.

"I'd do it for anyone."

"Oh," she said in a small voice. Roni bit her lip. "I need all the help I can get right now."

"I know that."

"No, it's something else. There's something I have to tell you, something terribly important," she whispered. "You can't tell anyone else. Zack, but Lisa was there. Lisa was in the car with me."

"Lisa?" Zack frowned, puzzled. "But you were alone when we found you."

"She ran away. But she was with me at the Roadhouse. Coming back in the car, we had a fight.

She grabbed the wheel and then . . ." Roni shuddered. The image of the stone wall looming in front of her was horribly real.

"But why? Why did she run away?"

"She's on probation. She was afraid of security, or the police finding her."

"Of course." Zack sighed. "That sounds like our Lisa," he said bitterly.

"I don't know what to do. What if she's hurt? What if she's delirious or something?"

"Don't worry," Zack said calmly. "I'll go tell Security."

"No! That's just it—you can't!" Roni cried. "I promised. It would be my fault if she got expelled, or charged with a crime."

Zack exploded again. "I don't believe you! Can't you see that Lisa isn't worth protecting? It's Lisa's own fault that she's on probation, and you're in enough trouble without lying to protect her."

"I can't tell, Zack," Roni pleaded. "She trusts me. She's my friend. . . ."

Zack let out an angry snort. "She left you pinned behind the wheel in a wrecked car, Roni. For all Lisa knew, you could have passed out again and died. Did you ever think about that?"

Shaken, Roni stared at him.

"I suggest you figure out what a friend really is before you go protecting anybody," Zack said curtly.

"She didn't mean to hurt me," Roni insisted. "She was scared. . . ."

"She nearly got you killed!" Zack clenched his hands, a look of disgust on his face.

"It was my fault, too. You have to find her," Roni insisted. "Find out where she is. She could be unconscious or something."

"If Security finds out you lied . . ."

"That's my problem, Zack. Don't tell them. Please try to find Lisa yourself."

Zack finally nodded. "You're right about one thing—we can't let her wander around if she's hurt. But I can't promise anything else."

Roni felt sick with worry. "Everything's gone so wrong. I'm in so much trouble." Tears welled up in her eyes again. "Don't hate me, Zack."

"I don't hate you. I told you, I'm mad at you because I care about you, because I was scared for you," Zack declared. "Don't you understand that?"

Roni nodded. "I was scared, too. Afraid of losing you. That's why I went with Lisa. I thought if you'd come meet me there, we'd be able to talk and everything would be all right."

Zack sat at her side. "What were you so scared of? I don't get it."

"Something happened."

"Since this afternoon? You were fine when I left you at the mailroom."

Roni laughed ruefully. "That was because I hadn't looked at my mail yet." She swallowed and took a deep breath. "I got my grades—Zack, I nearly flunked out. After everything I told you about being able to play hard and study hard . . . I . . . I was afraid to tell you after everything you said about not calling me because I wasn't serious enough for you."

Zack looked hurt. "You were afraid to tell me?"

Roni nodded. "I don't know what happened. I thought I was doing fine. I thought I aced those exams. Sam said . . ." Roni faltered. "Sam said I had to work harder in college."

"Oh, Roni." He put his arms around her. "You could have come to me. I would have helped you. We could even study together—I've taken some of the courses you're in. Please, ask me for help. I want you to come to me, not be afraid of me."

Roni grasped his shoulders. "But I was afraid. I thought you'd be disappointed in me. And see, now you are."

Roni hesitated. There was so much more to tell him. She wanted to be honest, but she was so scared. Maybe Zack could accept her bad grades and even help her, by studying with her. But he couldn't change what she'd done in Daytona. She had to tell him.

"There's more," she whispered.

"More secrets?" He almost laughed.

Roni felt sick to her stomach, but in a strange way she also felt too tired to lie anymore.

"After I got my grades, I was afraid to talk to you so I went to the suite. I needed to talk to Sam and Stacy, but instead we had a big fight. They were furious with me."

Zack started to say something, but Roni put her hand over his mouth. "Wait . . . wait until I finish." This was the hardest part of her confession. Zack was on her side now, but soon he might not be. She had to think carefully.

Finally, it all came out in a rush. "My father's not a senator, Stacy's is. And my father's not an alcoholic, either—that was my roommate Terry's dad. And it was her brother who got killed in the car accident."

Zack flinched. "Those things weren't true?"

"I don't know why I said all that. At the time it was a big joke, a game . . . to impress you and Lisa, I guess. It didn't seem to matter then, but it matters a lot now."

The look on Zack's face was a mixture of pain and surprise. Roni couldn't stand to see it. She had never felt like such a rat in her whole life.

"You made all that up? All that was a lie?" Zack's voice sounded mechanical.

"It all happened," Roni said, "but not to me. That's why Sam and Stacy were so hurt and angry, and I don't blame them." She couldn't even look Zack in the face.

"What an idiot I was," he said at last. "I really fell for it. I believed everything you said."

"Zack . . ." Roni reached out to him but he drew away.

"I remember when you told those stories," he said bitterly. "I thought I'd misjudged you. You seemed like such an airhead, but when I heard those terrible stories, I thought about what a hard life you must have had. It started to change the way I felt about you."

Roni felt faint. "You mean the only reason you liked me was because you felt sorry for me? What about now?"

"I don't know. You haven't told the truth about anything. How could I know how I feel about you?"

Zack's mouth was set in a grim line. "What do you want me to say, Roni?"

Her voice was pleading. "I'm not a liar, Zack. I've never lied about anything really important—about anything before this. Please, believe me. It was vacation and it just sort of happened. I didn't mean it. But the way I feel about you now, I can't stand the thought of losing you. Zack, please!"

He was silent. If their roles were reversed, Roni thought wildly, if he'd just told her the things she'd told him, she wasn't sure she could believe it either.

"I've ruined everything," she sobbed hopelessly.

"You're right," Zack said quietly. "You have."

Roni stared back at him, terrified. She really had lost him now.

"I'll find the nurse and get you out of here," Zack told her.

"And Lisa, will you find her? And . . . and tell me how she is?" Roni pleaded. "You don't have to care about me," she added, "just make sure Lisa's all right."

Zack closed his eyes as if she'd slapped him, then walked quickly away.

A minute later, the infirmary nurse flung back the curtain, bustling around Roni's bed. "I called your suite mates. They'll be waiting for the ambulance."

Roni sank against her pillow. "Ambulance?" she echoed vaguely.

"He'll take you to your room and you can sleep in your own bed tonight."

"That's good," Roni whispered. She couldn't bear being awake, remembering. All she wanted to do just then was sleep.

Chapter 13

Carl, the ambulance attendant, was a pleasant-looking guy not much older than Roni. Carefully, he rolled Roni's wheelchair up to the back doors of the ambulance.

"Wait, Carl," Roni told him. "Uh . . . I really feel pretty good. Couldn't I ride up front instead?"

"No way. Patients always ride in the back," he told her.

"But . . ." She could imagine being wheeled up to her dorm, attracting more attention than she wanted. "Couldn't I sit up front? I . . . I'll sign anything you want. Please? If I'm well enough to go to my room, I must be well enough to sit in the front seat."

Carl eyed her closely. "Riding in the ambulance is nothing to be embarrassed about."

Roni flushed. "But drunk driving *isn't* nothing to be embarrassed about."

They stared at each other. "Okay," Carl finally agreed. "You ride up front. But I'll walk you to your room."

"Of course," Roni agreed quickly. "That's only polite."

Some people were milling around in front of Rogers House, and they watched curiously as the ambulance pulled up. But when Roni climbed down clinging to Carl's arm as if he was her date, even managing a carefree laugh, they quickly lost interest.

"Are you doing okay?" Carl asked as they climbed the short flight of stairs to the second floor.

"Just scared," Roni answered. "My roommates—"

Carl nodded. "I heard it wasn't your car. Well, good luck."

Roni took a deep breath for courage. "Thanks."

"The nurse explained everything to your roommates on the phone. You'll be in good hands."

"I know." Roni paused outside the door, gathering her courage.

Then she cautiously pushed open the door to the suite. Sam and Stacy looked up immediately. Roni winced, unable to look either of them in the eye. At least no one else was there. She wouldn't have been able to stand it if the whole floor had gathered to stare and find out all the gruesome details.

Stacy sprang to her side, a look of alarm on her face. "You shouldn't be walking around alone! You sit right down."

"No," Sam declared, "she belongs in bed."

"Which do you want?" Stacy asked Roni anxiously.

Roni couldn't believe they were acting so concerned, but felt too weak to say anything. "Bed, please," she answered faintly.

They practically carried her into the bedroom and Roni collapsed gratefully on her bed.

"Stacy, I'm so sorry about your car. I'll pay for everything, I'll replace it."

"Will you forget about the car?" Stacy cried. "The nurse said you're supposed to rest and not worry."

Dumbfounded, Roni lay back as Stacy gently tucked a blanket over her legs. "You're not mad?"

Stacy rolled her eyes. "I'll manage without the car. I'm more worried about you!" For the first time, Roni noticed how pale Stacy looked. "We heard the car was totaled," Stacy said quietly. "And we were afraid you'd been . . . totaled, too."

"Me, too," Roni said in a small voice.

"Aren't you scared?"

"Terrified when I think about it," Roni admitted. "I'm trying not to."

"That's probably best," Stacy said, nodding. "You'll have plenty of time to think about it tomorrow or the next day."

"But the car," Roni repeated. "Will your insurance company cover it? What will your father say?" Roni glanced up anxiously, grateful and relieved that Stacy was making it so easy for her.

"We'll think about that tomorrow, too."

"I can't believe how nice you guys are being about this," Roni told her. "I'm so sorry . . . about everything. I wouldn't blame you if you hated me forever."

"I know you're sorry. And don't worry about criminal charges or any of that stuff," Stacy assured her. "I just want you to get well."

"And never to do anything that stupid again," Sam added.

"I won't, ever—I promise. I don't need another

warning like this," Roni said, swallowing hard. Tears were gathering in her eyes, and her throat felt full. She felt so grateful to her friends for being so wonderful. Even their anger was proof that they cared. Just like Zack. *Zack*. Thinking of the way they'd left things, Roni moaned softly.

"What is it? Your head?" Stacy bent anxiously over the bed.

Roni felt the tears slide down her cheeks. "It's Zack," she admitted. "He . . . he's pretty upset with me."

Stacy and Sam exchanged looks. "I know. He was here earlier," Stacy answered slowly. "He was pretty worried when you didn't show for your date."

"And angry," Sam said. "Zack seems like a good guy. And he cares an awful lot about you."

"You like him now? You didn't in Daytona." For some reason, Roni felt immensely pleased.

"I didn't exactly get to know him there, remember?"

Roni flushed. "I'm sorry. Will you guys ever forgive me?"

"Don't worry about that now," Stacy soothed.

"I was pretty hurt," Sam admitted, "but I guess no harm was done. I forgive you."

"I'll never do anything like it again!" Roni cried. If only they could believe her. "I . . . I know I have a lot to make up to you," she said sincerely. "To you, and to Zack." She twisted the blanket in her hands. "And I'll do it, too. I just hope he'll let me try."

"Get some rest," Stacy ordered. "All this can wait until morning."

Roni held out her hand. "Stacy, wait. Promise me that if Zack calls tonight you'll wake me up? I've got to talk to him. I've got to make things all right."

Stacy bent down, gently smoothing Roni's hair. "Get some sleep."

Stacy left the door partly open and Roni could hear her and Sam talking quietly in the living room. Her own mind was reeling. Zack . . . the stories . . . Lisa . . . the wrecked car—there was so much to think about, so much to straighten out.

Sunlight flooded the room, and Roni sat up in bed grasping the ends of the handknit shawl Sam had tucked around her shoulders.

"You look much better this morning," Sam told her from the chair where she was sitting. "And you seemed to sleep pretty well."

"Did you stay up and watch me sleep?" Roni stared at her roommate, incredulous.

"Stacy and I took turns," Sam admitted.

"You didn't have to do that. The doctor didn't tell you to, did he?"

"We wanted to."

Stacy entered, juggling three glasses and a container of orange juice. "Coffee will be ready in a minute." She yawned widely, setting everything down on Roni's bedside table. "No delirious ravings, I see," she said with a frown, imitating a doctor. "Let's check that pulse." She lifted Roni's wrist and held it up to her ear. Roni giggled.

"Thanks, Doctor Swanson." She tucked her wrist under the covers. "I'm really fine."

"You seem to be," Stacy said, sitting at the foot of

her bed. "You're completely alert, with none of the danger signs the doctor told us about."

"I feel much better. I would like my headache medication, though."

"Does your head hurt?" Sam bent over her, feeling her forehead for fever.

Roni smiled indulgently. "All I have is a tiny headache. No fever, though. Really, I'm all right."

A knock sounded on the outside door. Stacy went to see who it was. She looked like the cat that swallowed the canary when she came back into Roni's room. "Someone's here to see you."

Zack appeared behind her. He looked tense and rumpled, as if he hadn't gotten much sleep himself. Automatically, Roni smoothed her hair and pulled the shawl more tightly around her shoulders.

"I think we should leave you two alone." Stacy dragged Sam from the room.

"Hi," Roni said. Her voice sounded shrill.

Zack lingered by the door. "Are you okay?"

Roni nodded. "No fever or anything." She noticed his hair needed combing, but she still thought he was the most adorable boy she'd ever seen.

Zack closed the door. He sat down on the edge of Roni's bed, looking sheepish. "Roni about those stories . . . I remember now that you did try to talk to me seriously, that night at the library when we first got together. I just didn't want to hear it."

"That's right!" Roni cried, relieved. "I remember now. You wouldn't let me say anything about Daytona."

Zack nodded. "Also, I guess I can see that the stories were part of spring break. I mean, that atmosphere was crazy. I gave you a false impression of myself, too. Me as Mr. Party Animal—what a joke, huh?"

"It's not a joke," Roni said softly. "You work hard, and on vacations you play."

"It's as if I tricked you, though," Zack insisted. "I guess what I'm trying to say is that I'm not blameless in this. The way I acted down there was pretty stupid."

Roni felt so relieved she couldn't talk.

Zack took her hands in his. "When I think what might have happened to you last night—out there all alone . . ." He gathered her into his arms, kissing her hair and holding her tight. "I love you, Roni," he whispered. "I wasn't sure before, but last night I knew. If anything ever happened to you. . . ."

Roni lifted her face and he kissed her lips. When he pulled back, she managed to smile. Tenderly, Zack smoothed her hair and stroked her brow.

"I was a jerk, pretending not to like you, saying you were the wrong type. It's not true—you're exactly my type."

"Oh, Zack." She clung to him. Zack kissed her and her heart leaped happily. They still had some things to work out between them, but somehow Roni felt sure they were finally on a solid footing. They gazed at each other for a long while.

"*Lisa!*" Roni gasped suddenly. She grabbed Zack's hand eagerly. "What about Lisa?" she asked. "Did you find her last night? I was so worried."

"Don't be. She was in her dorm the whole time. We talked on the phone and she said she's okay, but she wouldn't let me see her. She also said that if you or anybody else told the police she was with you last night, she'd just deny the whole thing."

"I guess she's still scared."

"And pretty selfish," Zack retorted.

"Don't say that," Roni protested.

"Roni, she never even asked how you were."

"Oh," Roni said.

"She's putting you in a terrible spot, forcing you to lie."

"It will be all right." Roni tried to sound convincing. She wasn't so sure about it, though.

"Maybe she's not such a good friend," Zack said hesitantly. "Maybe she's too far gone to be anyone's friend."

"What do you mean?"

"I mean she's got a serious problem. I think she needs help, maybe even professional counseling. She cares more about booze than people." Zack took her hands in his. "Roni, in all the time I've known Lisa, I've never heard her have a serious conversation with anyone."

"That's not her fault," Roni protested. "You admitted it yourself—you liked her around for a good time, for vacations and parties. You didn't want her to be serious, and neither does anyone else. You can't blame her. You can't have it both ways."

Zack grew thoughtful. "I guess we've all treated her like that. But you and I were able to get past the good times, the vacation stories. We got close, but Lisa doesn't seem able to do that."

"I feel so badly, Zack." Suddenly Roni threw back her covers and swung her feet over the side of the bed.

"What are you doing? Get back to bed," Zack ordered.

Roni shook her head. "I'm going to see Lisa."

"You're not going anywhere."

Roni gave him her most determined look. "The doctor said I could get up when I felt ready. Well, I feel ready. I've got to see Lisa. I won't be able to rest if I don't."

"At least let me call the infirmary and see if it's okay," Zack proposed.

"If you have to," Roni replied. "But there is one thing you don't know about me yet, and it's that I'm awfully stubborn."

Zack laughed. "Are you kidding? When have you been anything *but* stubborn?"

Roni pulled out bureau drawers, tossing fresh clothes on the bed. Zack got up.

"Fine, go—but I'm going with you," he said.

Roni smiled. "Thanks."

"But the first sign that anything's wrong," Zack declared, "and I'm taking you straight to the doctor."

"Great. Now get out of here so I can get dressed."

A short time later, Roni and Zack approached Lisa's dorm room.

"You don't really have to do this, you know," Zack said.

"Yes, I do. I have to make sure she's okay."

"What if she won't talk to you? She wouldn't let me see her."

Roni hesitated. "I hadn't thought of that. Let me think for a minute." She scowled. "Hey, what if you pretend to be a delivery boy? Say you're delivering flowers or something, and when Lisa opens the door, I'll confront her."

"That's crazy," Zack protested. "Suppose she doesn't open the door?"

Roni shrugged. "I'll think of something, I suppose."

"Can't we do this a normal way? Do we have to have some crazy scheme?"

"Do you have a better idea?" Roni demanded.

"No," Zack admitted.

Reluctantly, he stood in front of Lisa's door while Roni flattened herself against the wall.

"You can do it," she whispered, giving him a thumbs-up sign.

Zack looked like he'd rather be anywhere but there, but he took a deep breath and then knocked loudly.

"Pizza for Lisa Evans," he called. Several girls passing in the hallway gaped at him. Zack colored but ignored them. "Lisa Evans? Open up!"

There was a scuffling sound behind Lisa's door. "Wha'?"

"Pizza!" Zack shouted. "Comes to eight seventy-five. Come on, hurry it up."

"Pizza? For breakfast?" Lisa grumbled. "I didn't order that. Go away."

Zack pounded even louder on the door. "Eight bucks, lady. I ain't leaving till I get it."

"Go away and leave me alone!" Lisa shouted angrily.

Zack looked at Roni to ask what to do next. Roni motioned for him to try one more time.

Sighing, Zack rapped his knuckles against the door, not once or twice, but a long, continuous tapping.

Suddenly Lisa's door flew open. "If you don't get out of here—"

Too late, Lisa realized it was a trick. She tried to slam the door, but Zack easily wedged his foot inside, forcing it open. Roni marched into the room. "Stand by the door, Zack," she commanded. "Don't let her get out."

Cornered, Lisa retreated to the window, sitting sulkily on the ledge. She was wearing a rumpled sweat suit and had pulled a bathrobe over that. Her thick dark hair hung wildly around her face, and there were dark smudges under her eyes where her makeup had rubbed off. Roni tried not to show how shocked she was at Lisa's appearance.

Lisa crossed her arms defensively. "I see you and Zack got back together. Everything worked out fine for you, as usual."

"We came over to make sure you're feeling okay."

Lisa stared at the single bandage on Roni's face, but didn't say anything.

"It's just a little cut," Roni said. "I have a minor concussion. I didn't know if you'd been hurt or not."

Lisa stared out the window. "I'm terrific, don't worry."

"Are you sure? No headache?"

"Of course I have a headache," Lisa snapped. "And one hell of a hangover."

Roni pursed her lips. "I mean besides that. Did you hit your head or anything? Thank God we had our seat belts on." She laughed. "Pretty crazy, huh?"

"You think this is funny?" Lisa glared at her. "Did you tell anyone I was there? Security? Anyone?"

"Of course not." Roni felt a stab of disappointment. Bitter tears filled her eyes, but she blinked them away. "I wouldn't do anything to hurt you, you know that. I wouldn't tell anyone."

"How kind!"

"Stacy's not pressing any charges, either," Roni continued. "She says her insurance will cover the damage. . . ." Roni faltered, unsure of what to say next.

"You know, I could sue you if I wanted," Lisa said. "You could have gotten me killed."

Shocked, Roni stared at her blankly. "Sue *me*?"

"I could be dead the way you were driving. You were out of control!"

"Of all the . . ." Zack swore angrily. "Let her try to sue and see how far she gets!" Disgusted, Zack pulled the door open. "C'mon, Roni, we don't need this."

"You would do that to me?" Roni asked, not moving.

"Ignore her," Zack advised. "Nobody's going to sue anybody. She'd have to go to court and admit how much she drinks, admit she practically forced you to go along with her. She could never sue you."

"Lisa didn't force me to do anything," Roni whispered.

Zack glared at Lisa. "She's forcing you to lie when you both should go to Security and tell the truth."

"What good would that do?" Lisa yelled. "I'm the

one who'd get in trouble, not Roni. Roni's rich father would just pay her way out of it, and I'd be the one who got blamed."

"We don't have to listen to this," Zack said, fuming.

Roni spoke quietly to Zack. "Wait for me in the hall, okay?"

"What?"

"I want to talk to Lisa alone. Wait outside, please?

"Are you sure?"

"Yes." she pushed him out the door and faced Lisa. "I know I'm not blameless in this, but I'm not out to get you either. Like it or not, I care about you."

"That's a surprise," Lisa sneered. "I thought you only cared about yourself."

"That's not fair and you know it. I'm your friend."

"You were my friend because you wanted to get to Zack," Lisa said bitterly. "If that's your idea of friendship, forget it." She raked her hands through her hair.

Roni felt ashamed. There was a grain of truth in what Lisa was saying. Feeling light-headed, she suddenly dropped onto the bed, dipping her head between her knees.

"Are you okay?" Lisa asked, looking alarmed.

Roni took a deep breath. "I'm fine," she said shakily.

Lisa sat back down, chewing her fingernails. "Look, why don't you just leave me alone, okay? I'll forget I ever knew you."

"Lisa, I'm so sorry," Roni said softly. "I don't want to hurt you. I want to help you."

"Spare me," Lisa said lightly. "You don't know what you want."

"Yes, I do."

Lisa laughed. "Don't kid yourself. You want to think you're this wonderful, responsible person, but you can't change. I know you, Roni. I've seen you in action. You're like me—you need excitement. There's never enough fun for you. I know—believe me."

Roni was shaken. Lisa had hit too close to home. Roni knew she was like that—or at least she had been for as long as she could remember.

Lisa grinned in satisfaction at Roni's worried expression. "You'll see," she said boldly. "You'll end up just like me."

Roni forced herself to sound confident. "No, I won't. I may like excitement, but I also need people—not just to go along with me—I need friends, Lisa, real friends—the kind that stick with you through good and bad."

"Get out," Lisa told her. "You're so sentimental it's sickening."

Roni stood up. "I'm going now, but if you ever need me, I'll be there for you."

"I won't need you. I won't need anyone!" Lisa shouted after her.

In the hall, Zack took Roni's arm. "You look terrible. I knew this would be too much for you. And she's not worth it."

Slowly, they left the dorm and headed back to Roni's suite. "It's so sad," she said. "She wanted to frighten me. She said we were alike, that I'd end up like her. Oh, Zack, I don't want that to happen." She searched his eyes.

Gently, Zack stroked her cheek. "You're not another Lisa. I'm not worried. You're stronger than her, Roni. You can be anything you want to be."

"Thanks, Zack." she squeezed his arm and smiled.

"The wall!—Watch out, the wall!" Roni woke up, arms thrashing against an imaginary enemy.

"You're okay," Sam was saying soothingly. "It was just a bad dream."

"More like a nightmare." Roni shook her head to clear away thoughts of the accident. "Did I sleep long?"

"All afternoon," Sam said, smiling softly.

"Here." Stacy came in and handed her a cup of tea. "Fresh from the pot. You look like you can use it more than me."

Roni accepted it gratefully. "I probably could."

"I guess your meeting with Lisa wore you out," Sam said diplomatically.

Roni grinned. "You guys deserve to hear everything." She patted the bed invitingly. "Lisa can be a tough act."

"I never thought she was genuine," Stacy declared. "But you wouldn't listen."

"You were right." Roni sighed.

Stacy shook her head sadly. "I feel sorry for her. She's got to be a very lonely person."

Roni looked at them both. "I'm scared," she admitted. "What if Lisa's right? What if I'm too far gone to change? I've been Roni the Party Girl so long. I'm not sure I can be anything else."

She stared out the window, cradling her teacup in both hands. "With Lisa, I never had to worry. We'd drink and get high. I knew I'd have fun if I drank enough."

"But Lisa's not having any fun now," Sam reminded her.

"I know. Like Zack said, the only thing she cares about now is booze." Roni set her cup down, her hands shaking. "That could have been me," she whispered.

"But you're different," Sam insisted, looking to Stacy for help. "Lisa doesn't seem to have any real friends, but you do."

"And you also have Zack," Stacy pointed out. "You're not such a hopeless case after all," she tried to tease.

Roni smiled weakly.

Stacy sat down beside Roni on her bed. "I think I understand," she said quietly. "I know what your life's been like. After all, mine wasn't so different. You learn to drink and party so young that it becomes a habit."

"That's it!" Roni cried. "It *is* a habit. I'm used to partying. I've always been good at it—acting wild and shocking people."

"I can't imagine you any other way," Stacy agreed.

"Yeah, can you see me as some dull bookworm?" Roni agreed. "My parents wanted me to be a dumb little debutante—an obedient little doll who never caused any trouble and fit right into the mold. You know: prep school, college, marriage, kids." Roni made a face. "Nothing about enjoying life, or finding out about myself or any special talents. I just couldn't stand to be that way."

"Especially when they made all the decisions for you," Stacy said. Roni nodded. "I know all about it."

"I have to be me," Roni declared strongly. "I can't do what other people tell me to do"—she grinned wryly—"unless, of course, it's for a good cause."

"You mean your punishment," Stacy said wisely.

Roni nodded. "I'm really lucky," she admitted. "I was terrified of my hearing, but the dean let me off pretty easy. Campus service is the best sentence I could have gotten."

"Yeah, you might even enjoy working at the campus outreach clinic," Sam pointed out.

"Imagine, me counseling other people." Roni sighed. "From party girl to social worker. I guess I might enjoy it, although I can't imagine making a career of it. Maybe I'll at least learn something that will help me get through to Lisa."

Sam laughed. "Roni, you've got so much energy. All you have to do is figure out a positive way to use it."

"You think that's it?"

"I know it is," Sam said, and Stacy nodded in agreement. "You just need direction, that's all."

"You're a whirlwind," Stacy added. "When you set out to do something, you get it done."

"That's true." Roni frowned. "But what should I do?"

"You'll have to figure that one out yourself," Sam admitted. "But meanwhile, don't sell yourself short. There's a lot in you to love."

"Zack knew that," Stacy reminded Roni.

"And I've always admired you," Sam told her.

"You have?" Roni was genuinely surprised. "Why?"

"Are you kidding?" Sam counted on her fingers. "You're not afraid of any challenge. You're gutsy and you follow through on things. You're loads of fun. And unpredictable! It's been a real eye opener, having you around."

"I feel that way, too," Stacy said. "We haven't said it a lot, but you really make things more exciting."

"Terry feels the same," Sam told her.

"I never knew that."

"You were a good person for her to room with. You taught her to loosen up, that work wasn't everything. I bet she's a lot happier now because of knowing you."

"You think so?" A smile spread over Roni's face, and she nodded gratefully. "You must be right. I must be a good person, because otherwise, you guys would never be friends with me. You guys are the greatest."

Chapter 14

It was one of those glorious afternoons in spring—
the kind that could make you feel like you'll burst
with happiness just for being alive. The air was
thick with the smell of flowers, and the sun was
strong. Roni unbuttoned her denim jacket as she
waited for Zack outside the community health
center. When she spotted his bright yellow sweater,
she bounded down the hill toward him.

Throwing her arms around his neck, she
squeezed hard.

"Whoa!" he cried with a laugh. "I thought you'd
be exhausted after such a hard day's work." He set
her on the ground.

"Not me," Roni bubbled. "I'm getting used to this
volunteer stuff. When I was sentenced to campus
service, I had no idea I might actually *enjoy* it."

Zack laughed, remembering how terrified Roni
had been the day of her hearing. "It's a lot better
than being expelled or suspended, that's for sure."

"Imagine, me of all people, learning to counsel
drug and alcohol abusers."

"Why not? You've got tons to offer them," Zack
said.

"Oh," Roni said as she pulled some pamphlets out of her purse. "I got these for Lisa."

"Lisa? Has she started speaking to you again?"

"Not a word," Roni confessed. "But I haven't given up on her. If she'd only read this stuff, she might get help."

"Don't count on it."

"I'm going to send these to her anyway, along with a personal note."

"She'll probably throw them out."

"I can always send more. Even if she doesn't keep them, at least she'll have to think about them."

They walked on in silence, holding hands and enjoying the warm, spring air.

"All set for tonight?" Zack asked.

"Completely. Imagine, throwing our first TGIF party together. And it's on a Saturday," she joked.

"Who cares what day it is, as long as you're my date?"

Linking arms, they strolled to the edge of the pond. "This is one party I really deserve," Roni commented. "I've never worked and studied so hard in my life. Lucky for you I like my tutor," she teased.

Zack flushed with pleasure. They had closed the library every night for the past two weeks. "You're learning a lot, though. Admit it," he teased back.

"About a lot of things," Roni confessed. "I'm learning that it's as much fun dancing with you all night as it ever was having a dozen strangers cut in."

Zack pretended to be offended. "You'd dance ith another man?"

"Just to keep you on your toes," Roni said with a giggle. "I can't change completely," she warned him.

Zack squeezed her happily. "I wouldn't want you to." He brushed a strand of hair away from her face. "I love you, Veronica Davies." Zack gazed into her eyes. "There's no one else like you, and there never will be."

She squeezed his hand and Zack bent to kiss her. Then his eyes widened and he smacked his forehead in dismay. "I almost forgot—I have to go pick up stuff for our TGIF party in town."

"You'd better get going."

Zack rushed away, then came back and put his arms around her again. "Almost forgot my good-bye kiss," he said. Roni kissed him, smiling contentedly.

"See you later, co-host?"

"Later, co-host."

Back in the suite, Roni got busy decoratng while Stacy finished the dusting. Sam had already mixed up batches of punch.

"There," Sam said, setting two large punch bowls on the coffee table. "All set to go: one straight fruit punch, one champagne punch."

"Sounds good." Roni picked up a huge bundle of dried flowers. The weekend before, she and Zack had found a wonderful old wooden crate on the sidewalk in front of a Chinese restaurant. Chinese calligraphy adorned the front and sides, and once Roni had scrubbed it down, it looked like a priceless antique. Carefully, she arranged the dried flowers and set the crate in the window.

"That looks fabulous," Sam said, surprised. There was a knock at the door. "That must be Maddie," she said. "She made batches of brownies for us."

"Fantastic!" Roni hurried to the door to greet Maddie.

"Wow! Fabulous dress!" she cried.

"Like it?" Maddie spun around. "It's from the forties. I found this great thrift shop in town."

"I know the one!" Roni cried. "As a matter of fact, that's where Zack and I got our outfits for tonight: matching sweaters from some college. They have big megaphones embroidered on the front."

"Oh, let me see," Maddie said enthusiastically.

Roni brought out her sweater and pulled it over her head. "Oh, no!" she gasped. "It's unraveling under the arm. I didn't even notice in the store!"

"So wear something else," Stacy suggested. "You've got tons of cute outfits."

"But then I won't match Zack! We planned it especially for tonight."

"Love," Stacy drawled sarcastically.

Maddie inspected the damage. "Don't flip out. I think I can save this. Do you have a crochet hook? Even a regular needle might do."

"I have a sewing kit," Sam said. "There'll be something there you can use."

"Great. I'll patch it for now. Later I can pick up these stitches to keep it from unraveling any more. You could get matching yarn to fix it with, and no one will ever know."

Roni sighed in relief. "You saved my life." She hung over Maddie's shoulder as she set to work.

Sam appeared holding up a bright turquoise sweat shirt. "Roni, you've inspired me. I'm going to call Aaron and have him wear his turquoise sweat shirt, too."

"But I have no one to call," Stacy wailed. "Pete's working until midnight."

"I'm sorry Stacy," Sam commiserated. "Maybe we could get you a stand-in."

"Forget it. I don't need desperation dates. What we need around here is another roommate ... someone like Terry—a nice reliable girl I can count on not to act like a sick puppy when she falls in love."

They all laughed.

"Actually," Roni mused, "I wouldn't mind a new roommate either. It's sort of lonely without Terry."

"Lonely? You're with Zack every second of the day."

"Not really. Besides, girl friends are special. You need both."

Sam glanced at Maddie, then looked quickly back to Roni. "Do you really think that?"

"Sure," Roni said. "But what can we do? Put an ad in the paper? I can see it now: 'Wanted, desirable stranger to room with nutty freshmen.'"

"What about asking someone we already know?" Sam continued slyly.

Maddie blushed and Roni's mouth dropped open in surprise. "Of course! Why didn't I think of that?"

Maddie looked up hopefully. "I've been dying to ask, but I couldn't."

"She wouldn't have to stay with her aunt anymore," Sam pointed out, "and we'd have a new roommate."

"I love it!" Roni exclaimed. "What do you think, Stace?"

Stacy grimaced. "Great, as long as she doesn't call me 'Stace' like you do."

"Never, I promise," Maddie swore.

Stacy grinned. "In that case . . ."

Maddie sprang up eagerly. "Are you sure, Roni? I'd be sharing your room. I mean, I'll understand if you have someone else in mind."

"No one but you. Besides, the more good study habits I'm surrounded by, the better. A brain like you will shame me into getting good grades."

Maddie reddened, but she laughed.

Sam clambered onto a chair. "Let's take a vote. I hereby nominate Madison Lerner as the new roommate of suite 2C."

"I hereby second the motion," Roni declared.

"Me, too." Stacy nodded.

"Then it's done." Roni gave Maddie a big hug. "Welcome, roomy."

Sam leaped from the chair, heading for the door. "I'm going to ask Pam what we have to do to make it official."

Maddie hastily pushed the sweater aside. "I should go with her."

"Sit," Roni commanded. "You have more important things to do. Let me try on this sweater and see if it's okay."

Stacy grinned. "This is what it's like living here,

Maddie. You'd better get used to it."

Maddie flashed a wide grin. "I don't think that's going to take long at all."

Here's a sneak preview of *Multiple Choice*, book number five in the continuing ROOMMATES series.

"I can't believe I did this," Maddie groaned, dropping her head onto her arms. "How could I be so stupid? What am I going to do?"

It was Wednesday night, and Maddie was frantic. Her paper was due in just over twelve hours, and all she had to show for her efforts were five scrambled pages of rambling, inconclusive comments about the use of prophecy in *Macbeth*. Her knuckles whitened as she gripped her pen, and she stared in disbelief at her work.

She lifted her head and looked wildly around the bedroom she shared with Roni. There was no sign of her roommate, who had disappeared on a mysterious errand with Zack shortly after dinner. Stacy, she knew, was in the ceramics studio working on a new project. For a moment, Maddie was so nervous she thought she was going to be sick to her stomach.

Taking a deep breath, she got up from her desk and crossed the room. Maybe Sam could help her. Sam was always so levelheaded, so reasonable, so sympathetic. Sam would know what to do.

The living room was empty, and there was no sound from the other bedroom. Her hope sinking, Maddie opened the door and poked her head in. Sam was gone.

Feeling utterly alone, Maddie walked over to Sam's bed and dropped down onto it, gripping the bedspread with her hands and closing her eyes. She had to stay calm, or she would never get this paper done by morning. As she opened her eyes, she looked bleakly around the room, hoping that Samantha would suddenly materialize and help her out of this crisis. Finally, out of curiosity, her eyes came to rest on Sam's desk.

Maddie clenched her teeth and walked dejectedly over to where Sam's typewriter sat. Next to it, neatly covered in a clear plastic folder, was Sam's paper. After a quick glance into the living room, Maddie picked it up and read through the opening paragraph. Without question, all the long hours Sam had labored over her paper had paid off. The main theme of the paper was well thought out and very interesting. Maddie read on.

Twenty pages later she lowered Sam's Shakespeare paper and stared blindly into space. There was absolutely no way she could write that good a paper in one night—and that was what Professor Harrison expected. She groped for the chair and pulled it out, lowering herself into it like a feeble old woman.

"What am I going to do?" she repeated aloud. Never in her life had she ever felt so lost and helpless. Never in her life had she failed to do a superior job on a school assignment. And now, she had failed to do it at all. Period.

Her blank gaze focused on a hastily scribbled note on the desk. It was in Stacy's handwriting. "Sam—Aaron called—he said to meet him at eight for the rally—he has to be there earlier than he thought."

The rally. Maddie shook her head, trying to figure out what that meant. And then it came back to her. Sam's boyfriend had helped to organize a political rally about runaway defense department spending, and Sam had been talking for days about the speakers they had lined up. It was scheduled for that night, and was expected to last several hours. Sam would be gone until at least ten–thirty.

Almost hypnotized, Maddie watched herself stand up with Sam's paper in her hand and cross to the door. If she stopped to think about it, she couldn't go through with it. But if she didn't do it, she'd fail the class, and that was something she just couldn't afford to do. She hurried to her own room and grabbed her wallet, and then slipped out of the suite, heading for the library—and the copying machine on the first floor.

Roommates

We hope you enjoyed reading this book. If you would like to receive further information about titles available in the Bantam series, just write to the address below, with your name and address: Kim Prior, Bantam Books, 61–63 Uxbridge Road, Ealing, London W5 5SA.

If you live in Australia or New Zealand and would like more information about the series, please write to:

Sally Porter
Transworld Publishers
(Australia) Pty Ltd.
15-23 Helles Avenue
Moorebank
N.S.W. 2170
AUSTRALIA

Kiri Martin
Transworld Publishers (NZ) Ltd
Cnr. Moselle and Waipareira
Avenues
Henderson
Auckland
NEW ZEALAND

All Bantam Young Adult books are available at your bookshop or newsagent, or can be ordered from the following address: Corgi/Bantam Books, Cash Sales Department, PO Box 11, Falmouth, Cornwall, TR10 9EN.

Please list the title(s) you would like, and send together with a cheque or postal order. You should allow for the cost of the book(s) plus postage and packing charges as follows:

All orders up to a total of £5.00: 50p
All orders in excess of £5.00: Free

Please note that payment must be made in pounds sterling; other currencies are unacceptable.

(The above applies to readers in the UK and Republic of Ireland only)

B.F.P.O. customers, please allow for the cost of the book(s) plus the following for postage and packing: 60p for the first book, 25p for the second book and 15p per copy for the next 7 books, thereafter 9p per book.

Overseas customers, please allow £1.25 for postage and packing for the first book, 75p for the second book, and 28p for each subsequent title ordered.

Thank you!